"Lucy, you kiss me good-

As if he'd uttered an obscenity, every one of the men was staring at him. "Why would she do that?" the bald one blurted.

"She's my wife," Troy announced with a bland smile. "Who else would she kiss good-morning?"

For a wild moment he thought Lucy was going to dump the coffeepot and its contents over his head. "We're separated," she said. "We're going to get a divorce."

"So is that your decision?"

Her eyes blazed into his. "Yes."

"Ah...in that case you won't mind if I hang around for a few days. Obviously, if you're going to divorce me, my presence shouldn't matter to you one way or the other."

"You ought to be down on your knees giving thanks that this is a coffeepot and not a carving knife," she grated. "Stop being insufferable, Troy, and go back to Vancouver."

Dear Reader,

Welcome to the second of three scintillating books by Sandra Field. When Sandra first came up with the idea for *Beyond Reach* (#1806) she fell in love with her characters so much that she couldn't bear the thought of leaving them behind. So she wrote another book. Then another.... And SIGNIFICANT OTHERS was born.

"This series of three books crept up on me unawares. After Troy and Lucy met in the West Indies, I found myself curious to discover how marriage would change them. Hence *Second Honeymoon*, again set on an island, this time off the coast of Nova Scotia. Lucy's laid-back friend Quentin and her uptight sister Marcia played minor roles in *Second Honeymoon*. Once Quentin had appeared on the scene, I knew I wouldn't rest until I'd brought him face-to-face with Marcia, which I did in my next book, *After Hours*."

Though all three books can be read on their own, why not follow Marcia and Quentin's own romance in *After Hours*—coming soon in Harlequin Presents! Look for the special SIGNIFICANT OTHERS flash at your favorite bookstore—this is one series you don't want to miss!

Happy reading!

The Editor

SANDRA FIELD

Second Honeymoon

Harlequin Presents first edition

ISBN 0-373-11830-4

First North American Publication 1996.

Copyright © 1995 by Sandra Field.

Harlequin Books

TORONTO • NEW YORK • LONDON
AMSTERDAM • PARIS • SYDNEY • HAMBURG
STOCKHOLM • ATHENS • TOKYO • MILAN
MADRID • WARSAW • BUDAPEST • AUCKLAND

ISBN 0-373-11830-9

SECOND HONEYMOON

First North American Publication 1996.

CHAPTER ONE

UNTIL four that afternoon, it was a day like any other.

At four o'clock Troy Donovan strode past the receptionist's desk, giving Vera a distracted smile and quite oblivious to the fact that the eyes of every woman in the room had swiveled to follow his progress.

Vera smiled back. "Your mail's on your desk," she said. Vera was very happily married to a civil servant who adored her, but she had long ago decided that the woman who could ignore the cleft in Dr Troy Donovan's chin, not to mention the breadth of his shoulders and his sexy gray eyes, might as well be in her coffin. How his wife could have left him was more than Vera could imagine.

"Thanks, Vera." Troy marched down the corridor—enjoying the stretch in his long legs after the hours he'd spent in the operating room, rubbing at the back of his neck under the collar of his open-necked shirt. He was supposed to be at a meeting at four-thirty. He'd have time to glance at his mail and make a few phone calls first. He pushed open the door of his office and shuffled through the neat pile of envelopes on his desk.

The letterhead on a white vellum envelope leaped out at him. The institute whose name was printed in ornate script on the envelope was located in Arizona, and was the most prestigious center in the continent for pediatric plastic surgery—Troy's speciality. But why would they be writing to him? Slowly he sat down at his desk and reached for his letter-opener.

Ten minutes later Troy was still staring at the thick sheet of vellum. He was being offered a job. A plum job. A prize job. The very pick of the crop. A job that any craniofacial surgeon in the world would yearn after. Teaching, surgery, opportunities for research—it was all there, and at a salary that made him blink.

A new start. A new country, a new hospital, a whole group of new people. None of whom would know about Lucy or Michael.

He could sell the house where he and Lucy had lived during the four brief years of their marriage. Where he had stayed by himself for the twelve months since she had gone. Sell it. Be rid of it and all its memories. Start afresh.

He buried his head in his hands, feeling the long-familiar pain rip at his guts. Twelve months since she had left him, and not for one day of those months had he been without her presence. It walked down the hospital corridors beside him. Perched on the stool by the west window in the kitchen, the evening sun burnishing the mahogany curls. It lay alongside him in the big bed where they had taken such pleasure in each other.

Why move to another country? He'd only take her with him.

Jarring as an electric shock, the telephone shrilled in his ear. Automatically he picked up the receiver. "Donovan speaking."

Vera said, "There are two people here to see you if you have a minute, Dr Donovan. Trish and Peter Winslow. They do realize they don't have an appointment."

Troy remembered them instantly. Two years ago their little girl had sustained third-degree burns, and had—mercifully, in his opinion—died. Pushing the letter from

Arizona to one side, he said, "Send them in, please, Vera."

Trish came in first, her blue eyes smiling; the last time Troy had seen her they had been filled with desolation. Her husband Peter, raw-boned and inarticulate, followed her. With a nasty jolt in his chest Troy saw that Peter was carrying a baby.

Trish said shyly, "We were here for my six-week checkup and we wanted to come and see you... We've never forgotten how kind you were. We thought you'd like to know we have a new baby; we called her Sarah. Show him, Peter."

Peter came round the desk, bumping into a chair on the way; for all his clumsiness, he made intricately carved pine furniture that won awards at the local craft fairs. He proffered the baby rather as if she were a chunk of wood.

Every nerve protesting, Troy took the small bundle in his arms. Sarah, disturbed by the transition, opened smoke-blue eyes, yawned, and fell asleep again. Her dimpled fist and the tiny ovals of her fingernails were perfectly formed and perfectly beautiful. Not sure he could trust his voice, Troy said tritely, "She's lovely. You must be very happy."

"Yes." Trish's smile included her husband. "No one can ever replace Mandy, but we needed a new start— didn't we, Peter?"

The very words that he himself had used, Troy thought numbly.

Peter rubbed his jaw, staring at the desk rather than at Troy. "You were straight with us, Doc," he said. "I don't like anyone tryin' to hide the knotholes from me. Doesn't do any good in the long run; you find 'em anyway. You never did that. Not once."

Sarah whimpered in her sleep. Troy said—and at one level it was true—"I'm very happy for both of you, and I wish you and the baby all the best... Here, Peter, you'd better take her before she starts to cry. And do sit down, please."

"You got kids, Doc?"

"No," Troy said. It was the simplest answer, the easiest; yet he hated himself for making it. He tried to pay attention, because Trish was telling him about the addition Peter had built on their bungalow and about the crib he had hand-carved for Sarah.

Then she said, "We must go. I know you're always so busy. I hope things are going as well for you as they are for us."

She clearly had no knowledge of his personal life. Troy said heartily, "Fine, thanks, Trish. I'm really glad you dropped in. And it was a pleasure to have met Sarah."

As the door closed behind them he let out his breath in a long sigh and wandered over to the window. Above the downtown highrises soared the peaks of Grouse and Seymour Mountains, where he and Lucy had often skied together. It was an enviable view and he didn't even see it. Trish and Peter's marriage had held firm under the onslaught of tragedy, he thought heavily, and they'd had the courage to bring a second child into a world that they knew all too well could be both cruel and capricious.

Trish and Peter had done better than he and Lucy. They'd earned their new start.

He'd take the job, he thought fiercely. Take it and get the hell out of here. It couldn't be any worse in Phoenix than it was in Vancouver, and it might well be better—at least there'd be no memories of Lucy there. He'd get out more, too, start dating on a regular basis—maybe remarry.

To remarry he'd have to divorce Lucy.

Divorce Lucy? The idea was ludicrous.

With a low growl of frustration Troy picked up the sheaf of notes Vera had collected for the meeting and left his office. And if he was more than usually intolerant of the bureaucratic bunglings and asinine government cutbacks that were part and parcel of all the hospital meetings nowadays, he wasn't about to apologise to anyone for his bad temper.

The meeting ran late. Troy hurried back to his office and changed from the casual cotton trousers and shirt that he wore around the hospital into a gray business suit and a formal white shirt. After adjusting his silk tie in the mirror he ran a comb through his hair. Because it was blond and thick, and streaked by the sun, no one but Troy would have noticed the few gray hairs over his ears. He knew they were there, though. After all, he was thirty-seven years old.

He'd be forty soon. If he was going to make a new start, he'd better get a move on.

He read the letter from the institute once again. That they were offering him the job before they opened it for competition was to say the least flattering. The letter concluded with the polite hope that they would hear from him by the first week of September.

First thing tomorrow he'd get Vera to fax them. He should fly down there and check the situation out before making a decision. He had three weeks' vacation starting next week, and while he'd tentatively arranged to go sailing with his long-time friend Gavin for about ten days he could cancel out of that with no difficulty. The timing was ideal.

And if he was into new starts, Troy thought, tucking his wallet in his inner pocket, he did have a date tonight.

A bona fide date with the female ophthalmologist who'd set the eye clinic on its heels when she'd arrived from Montreal six months ago.

Dr Martine Robichaud was intelligent, beautiful and sophisticated, and a brilliant diagnostician to boot. And, unless he was misreading all the signals, she was in serious pursuit of him. While this was their third date he had yet to touch her, other than a casual hand on her elbow, an arm around her shoulders to adjust her raincoat. Maybe tonight he should change that, too. It was time—past time—that he quit being incapacitated by the past. Time to let go of the woman who no longer wanted him and to find one who did.

He gave himself a defiant grin in the mirror, picked up his car keys and ran down the stairs to the parking lot. He was meeting Martine at a bar on Robson Street at seven; he'd better hurry.

He got there five minutes before her, and thus had the pleasure of watching her walk across the room toward his table. Heads turned; conversation stilled. She was, he sensed, both aware of this and unaffected by it. He stood up, rested both hands on her shoulders—rediscovering with a small shock how much shorter than he she was—and kissed her cheek. Contradicting the tailored linen dress and classic gold jewelry, her scent was complex, sensual—even a touch flamboyant.

He was quite sure the contrast was deliberate. With a twinge of excitement he pulled out her chair, watching the swing of her straight dark hair, the grace of her movements, and was not surprised when the waiter came to their table as soon as she was seated.

"Extra dry martini, no olive, please," she said in her impeccable English, which was flavored with the slightest of accents from her Francophone heritage. "I'm sorry

I'm late, Troy. Another of these cutback meetings—they manage to cut back on everything but my time.''

He smiled at her. ''I behaved disgracefully at the surgery meeting. Not that it'll make any difference.''

They talked easily about hospital matters, then moved to the trip Martine had taken to San Francisco and the conference Troy had attended in Texas. And all the while Troy was aware that the whole conversation was window-dressing—interesting, urbane and witty, most certainly, but window-dressing, nevertheless.

When they had almost finished their second drink, he said casually, ''Shall we move on? I thought we might have dinner at the new place on Granville Island that everyone's raving about.''

''Or,'' Martine said, ''we could go to my apartment.''

Her dark brown eyes were unwavering, her purpose clear. ''You're very direct,'' Troy said.

''I almost always know what I want.''

He looked down at his hands. A couple of months ago he had tried taking off his wedding-band and putting it away in his bureau, and had found himself unable to do so. So he had compromised, and now wore it on his right hand. ''Technically I'm still married,'' he replied. ''Even though I haven't lived with my wife for the last year. Do you know that, too?''

She nodded. ''I noticed you the very first time we met at the general staff meeting. So I checked out your marital status and was told you were separated. At the time, I have to admit, you seemed only half-alive. Then one day in the canteen I saw you laugh out loud at something someone had said, and that's when I knew I wanted to go to bed with you. The difference was as day to night.''

"You see me as a challenge, in other words," he said drily.

"I am not promiscuous," she said, and put down her glass.

"I never thought you were," Troy responded, and realized it for the truth. Her offer was, in its way, as flattering as that from the institute in Arizona.

Lucy might not want him, but other people did, he thought with sudden underlying fury, and drained his own glass. "Let me drive you to your car, then I can follow you to your apartment."

Fifteen minutes later he was standing in Martine's living-room. It exhibited the same cool, uncluttered elegance as the woman herself, although the great jug of vivid silk peonies in one corner hinted at climes other than coolness. She had poured him a drink and then excused herself; he took a big gulp of an exquisitely smooth malt whiskey, and wished he didn't feel so much like a teenager on his first date.

The room was warm. He took off his jacket and loosened his tie, and prowled around looking at the serigraphs on the pale pink walls and the books on the shelves—all of which demonstrated a taste both individualistic and eclectic. Why, then, did he feel so hollow inside?

From behind him Martine said lightly, "Have you read the latest Atwood? I always buy her books in hardcover because I can't wait for the paperback."

He hadn't come here to talk about Canadian literature. Troy turned around. She had shed the linen dress in favor of a flowing black jumpsuit that revealed her creamy shoulders and clung to her hips. In the soft light of the single lamp her eyes and her hair also looked black. He said flatly, "Where's your bedroom?" and pulled off his tie, flinging it on the plump leather couch.

Her lashes flickered. "This way," she said.

She had lit a candle on either side of the wide bed, and had pulled back the covers. The room looked like a stage set, Troy thought. Seduction Scene—take one. He began unbuttoning his shirt with furious haste.

Martine murmured, "There's no hurry; we have all night."

"I haven't been with anyone except my wife since the day I met her," Troy said, noticing with a distant part of his mind how he was avoiding the use of Lucy's name in this room.

"Ah...then I am flattered."

He didn't like Martine using the same word he had used in his thoughts. Quit thinking, for God's sake, he told himself. This isn't about your brain, it's about your genitals. You're going to break out of the cage you've been in for what seems like forever. So get on with it.

As he hauled his shirt out of his waistband Martine ran her fingers up his chest and raised her face for his kiss. Without finesse he pulled her close to his body and began kissing her—hard, almost angry kisses. With one hand he stroked her hair—its smoothness another shock—and with the other found the rise of her breast under the sensuous black fabric.

And somehow, in the confusion of desperation, incipient desire and raw novelty that was tumbling through his brain and his body, Troy knew that he had expected to find the full curve of Lucy's breast—so familiar, so desirable—not the small, firm peak of another woman's. A woman who was a stranger to him.

A woman who wasn't Lucy.

His hand felt like a lump of ice. Or was it his heart that felt that way? With an inarticulate groan he pulled his mouth free, let go of Martine and sat down hard on the corner of the bed, running his fingers through his hair and realizing dimly that the harsh breathing he was hearing was his own.

Resting his hands on his thighs, because his fingers were trembling and he didn't want Martine to see that, he said hoarsely, "I'm sorry...more sorry than I can say. I can't make love with you, Martine. I just...can't."

"You're still in love with your wife."

He glanced up. Her voice had been level, her face was expressionless, and he had no idea what she was thinking or feeling. Both were well hidden, he thought, with a stab of entirely irrational rage. "I don't know the answer to that. If I am, I'm a damn fool."

"What is her name?"

"You mean no one's told you about her?"

"I endeavor not to listen to gossip," Martine said coolly, crossing her arms over her chest. "I only asked about your marital status for my own protection."

"Her name's Lucy."

"Why did she leave you? Because I am presuming the separation wasn't of your choice."

"You got that right," Troy said, more bitterly than he'd intended, reaching for his shirt where it had fallen on the carpet and shrugging into it. He hated talking about Lucy, but he owed Martine, minimally, the decency of an explanation. "Can we go back into the living-room?"

"Better than that. We will go to the kitchen and I will make an omelette," Martine said composedly.

For the first time since he had entered the apartment, Troy really looked at her. "You're not surprised by what happened," he said slowly. "Or rather, didn't happen."

"No. But I thought you worth the risk."

"Playing games with me, Martine?"

She gave a very Gallic shrug. "Wanting you in my bed—that's all."

Discovering that he thoroughly disliked someone else anticipating his reactions before he knew them himself, Troy said, "Why weren't you surprised?"

"Not long ago I overheard three of the nurses in the laser clinic bemoaning the fact that you never dated anyone. Since I saw no overt signs that you were homosexual, I could only assume you didn't feel yourself to be free."

He had been more than competently diagnosed; trying to shrug off his distaste, both for Martine's objectivity and her accuracy, he said, "I can't believe you want me so badly that you'd risk the kind of rejection I just subjected you to—and no, I'm not fishing for compliments."

"Then you'll get none." She widened her dark eyes. "A Spanish omelette?" she asked.

"To really put the lid on my lack of romantic sensibility, I'm extremely hungry," Troy said in faint surprise. "Why don't we blow our cholesterol counts and make it a six-egg omelette?"

"Four," she said, leading him into a kitchen that looked dauntingly efficient. "Three for you and one for me." Opening the massive refrigerator, she put red and green peppers and a bunch of green onions on the counter. "You may chop these. Very fine."

Obediently Troy did as he was told. As the small heap of red and green cubes accumulated he heard himself say, "I was offered a job today in Arizona."

"Ah? Tell me about it." After he had given her the details, she said, "And will you take it?"

"I plan to go down and check it out."

"So is this another rejection?"

The oversize apron she had tied round her waist made her look more human, more approachable. He put the knife down and said straightforwardly, "Martine, it's clear to me—and must be to you as well—that I'm not ready for an affair. Serious or otherwise. Nor do I really want to bare my soul and tell you all about the breakdown of my marriage."

Moodily he pulled at the rubber bands from the bunch of onions. "I need to get away. Out of Vancouver. Away from nurses who think I should be dating—away from everyone who knew Lucy and me as a couple in the days when I was happy... I need a new start. And Arizona might very well give me that."

"You'd be missed," Martine said obliquely.

The thought that she might possibly be falling in love with him filled Troy with dismay. "For a while I might be missed. But not for long. No one's irreplaceable."

"Not even Lucy?" she flashed with the first show of temper he'd seen.

Her question flicked him on the raw. And, of course, he had no answer for her. "Shall I chop all these onions?" he said evenly.

"Half would be plenty." Whisking the eggs vigorously, she added, "I've never married, Troy. I'm beginning to feel it's time I did. Particularly if I want a child."

The knife in his hands didn't even falter. "You're an exceptionally attractive woman. Any number of men would find it a privilege and an adventure to be married to you."

"But not you."

"No, Martine. Not me."

She banged the bowl of eggs down on the counter so hard that the yellow liquid swirled to the rim. "Later on I'll no doubt be grateful that we had this conversation. That you didn't take me to bed. But for now I feel anything but grateful."

Troy was damned if he was going to feel guilty; as far as he was concerned he hadn't done one single thing to encourage her to fall in love with him. Quite suddenly the stark, efficient kitchen, the perceptive and beautiful woman glaring at him across the expanse of countertop, the false domesticity of the scene, were all too much for him. He said, "Martine, why don't we skip the omelette? I suspect neither one of us is in the mood for food or small talk—and we seem to have said anything else there is to say."

"Fine," she snapped. "You can see yourself out."

He stood up and said truthfully, "If I've done anything to hurt you that wasn't my intention, and I'm sorry. Goodnight."

Grabbing his jacket and tie on his way through the living-room, he flicked the lock on the door and stepped out into the corridor. The door shut smartly behind him. He chose the stairs rather than the elevator, taking them two at a time and feeling rather like a little boy let out of school.

He'd learned one thing this evening. He wasn't ready for any kind of emotional involvement.

It wasn't until Troy unlocked his own front door and stepped into the house where he'd lived with Lucy that his new-found sense of freedom evaporated. Although Lucy's clothes were gone from the front closet, although

her scent no longer lingered in the hallway and her voice
didn't call a welcome from upstairs, her stamp was
everywhere—in every corner of the house.

He walked across the hall and stood in the doorway
of the living-room. It wasn't an elegant room, like
Martine's, but it was full of color and unexpected
treasures—ranging from the seashells Lucy had collected in the Virgin Islands, where they had met, to a
collection of Tibetan singing-bowls they had found in a
bazaar in India. She had had a brief craze for embroid-
ering cushions, the rather uneven results of which were
lying on every chair, and the vibrant, Impressionistic
watercolor she had fallen in love with in Provence, and
which he had taken enormous pleasure in buying for her,
hung over the fireplace.

Nothing matched; Troy knew that—an interior dec-
orator would have thrown up her hands in despair. But
somehow the room was redolent of Lucy's warmth and
love of life.

He didn't want Martine. Or anyone else like Martine.
He wanted Lucy.

In his mind's eye he could picture the rest of the house
very easily. The kitchen had never been Lucy's favorite
room, although she could make cheesecakes that melted
in the mouth and she liked stir fries because no two ever
came out the same. She had never used the copper pans
that hung from the ceiling; rather, she had loved the way
the sun shot turquoise fire from them late in the
afternoon. The bathroom she had decorated in forest-
green and scarlet as soon as they had moved in, because,
she had said, every day with him felt like Christmas Day.

The bedroom, for the sake of his sanity, he had
stripped of all her touches.

Reluctantly Troy came back to the present, to the reality of a house empty but for himself and his memories. As though pulled by an unseen hand, he walked upstairs and into the den. The photographs that had been in the bedroom were now in here. Lucy's face laughed at him from within a gold frame on the bookshelves and in the informal snapshot on the pine desk her arms were wrapped around him, the blue waters of the Virgin Islands tingeing her eyes with the same vivid blue, her tangled mahogany curls standing out from her head like an aureole. Tall, beautiful Lucy, who, when she had married Troy, had made him happier than he had thought it was possible to be.

And then, side by side on the shelf, there were the photos of Michael.

Michael, their son. Who had died when he was seven months old, a year and a half ago. Who was the reason Lucy had left Troy alone in the big house on the bay.

Blond curls, eyes the same color as Sarah's, and a toothless grin that bespoke Michael's delight in the world in which he had found himself.

Troy turned on his heel and left the room, passing the door to the nursery as he went—a door that remained closed all the time. He walked downstairs again, his footsteps echoing in the hall, and in the kitchen took a pizza out of the freezer and thrust it in the oven. Shoving his hands in his pockets, he went to stand by the window, where the trees' serrated black edges cut into a star-spattered sky, and was achingly aware of the silence of the house, of his solitude and his loneliness.

He was in limbo. Nowhere. Alone yet unable to be with anyone. Divorced from laughter and the small, cumulative pleasures of living with the woman he loved.

Cut off from his sexuality and the deep erotic joy he had found in Lucy.

He was thirty-seven years old.

He wanted another child. He had loved being a father, and the thought of remaining childless filled him with a nameless dread. All too well as he stood there he could recall Sarah's tiny movements, and her miniature perfection as she had lain trustingly in his arms. He wanted a family. Like sex, this was a normal enough human urge. Yet Lucy was denying him both of them.

He moved his shoulders uneasily. The job he'd been offered today wouldn't interest him nearly as much if Lucy were still living with him. He knew that as well as he knew that the sun would rise in the morning. He loved his present job—was more than fulfilled and challenged by it in every hour he spent in the hospital.

So yet another thing that had been stolen from him was decisiveness. He was allowing his future career to depend on Lucy. He'd never sold the house they'd lived in because he kept hoping she'd come back to it. He couldn't even take a lover, for God's sake.

What kind of a man was he?

An empty shell, like the whelks and angel wings Lucy had scattered round the living-room.

So what the hell was he going to do about it? Eat frozen pizza in a house that held nothing but memories for the rest of his life? Stay celibate because no other woman was Lucy?

It was five months since he'd seen her. Last April he'd flown to Ottawa, where she was living, and pleaded with her to come back to him. White-faced, she'd refused. And like a beaten dog he'd crawled back home, only wanting privacy to lick his wounds.

Dammit, he thought, that's not good enough. Once, years ago, she'd told him that there was no use begging anyone for anything. So why had he wasted his time begging her for something she didn't want to give? He'd never do that again. Never.

His mind made another leap. Maybe, Troy thought, he was kidding himself that he was still in love with her. If he saw her again he might realize that he was clinging to something that existed only in his imagination: a prettified notion of undying love, a romantic fantasy that had no basis in reality.

Like a limpet glued to its rock, he was still clasping the words he'd said on their wedding-day, and had meant with all his heart. "Til death us do part". Death had parted them, all right. Though not quite in the way the marriage ceremony had pictured it.

Could it be true? Might he discover, if he saw Lucy, that the ties binding him to her had unraveled of their own accord? Or even rotted from disuse, thereby freeing him?

He didn't know the answers to his own questions. He did know he was sick to death of being half a man, a hollow man, a man of straw. He was tired of feeling frustrated, trapped and unhappy... How long before his friends got bored with him, before women like Martine started viewing him as a crabby old bachelor who was better avoided?

The buzzer rang on the oven. Troy shoveled the pizza on to a plate and sat down at the counter. He chewed the crust and the layered cheese and mushrooms as if they were cardboard, his convictions—and his anger—hardening.

He was going to go and see Lucy. And this time he'd tell her she could come back and be his wife—in fact as well as in name—or else he'd file for a divorce. A simple choice. Yes or no.

No more begging. No more opening himself to the kind of rejection he'd suffered in April. No more of the dull ache that had lodged itself in his belly months ago and never gone away. He was through with being a zombie. Enough was enough.

Marriage or divorce. A straightforward choice. And then he'd know where he was, even if he didn't like it very much. Because the hard fact was that Lucy, in the year since she had stormed out of the house after the worst fight in their marriage, had not once gotten in touch with him. No phone calls, no letters, not even a Christmas card.

Divorce. Troy played with the word in his mind, hating the very sound of it, yet knowing he'd be a naïve fool to imagine that Lucy was going to throw herself in his arms the minute he walked across the threshold of her apartment. There was a very strong possibility she might slam the door in his face.

If she chose—for the third time—to reject him, then somehow he'd have to learn to let go of her. With the sharpest of scalpels he'd have to amputate her from his body and his soul, and afterwards he'd have to allow himself to recuperate, to heal, so that he could rebuild a life that would include risk and intimacy and, eventually, children.

But in order to let go of her, he had to see her first.

The pizza seemed to have disappeared. Troy poured himself a beer, grabbed the latest medical journal and went upstairs to read it.

Troy slept better that night than he had in weeks, and the next morning his resolve was unchanged. He was going to get on with his life, Lucy or no Lucy. And the sooner he saw her, the better. It had, however, occurred to him that before he went banging on the door of her apartment it might be sensible to check that she hadn't gone away on holiday. So that afternoon he phoned Evelyn Barnes, his mother-in-law, who also lived in Ottawa.

"Troy here. How are you, Evelyn?"

With genuine pleasure Evelyn said, "How nice to hear from you. I'm snowed under at work and otherwise fine."

Evelyn was a forensic pathologist; while she lacked the emotional warmth of her middle daughter, Lucy, Troy had always known she was fond of him, and that she had been upset when Lucy had left him. He said, "Is Lucy around? While I'd rather you didn't warn her ahead of time, I need to see her."

Evelyn hesitated. "No...no, she hasn't lived in Ottawa since May."

She's found another man.

The words had sprung from nowhere, and the rush of emotion that churned in Troy's chest had nothing to do with detachment. "You mean she's moved?" he said stupidly.

"She's working on the east coast for the summer."

So it was temporary. Troy loosened his hold on the receiver. "When'll she be back?"

"Not until October, as far as I know."

It was now the end of August. Suffused with an anger that he made no attempt to subdue, Troy said, "I can't wait that long. Give me her address and I'll go wherever she is."

The pause was longer this time. Evelyn said reluctantly, "She made me promise not to tell you her whereabouts."

"For Pete's sake," he exploded, "what's she playing at?"

"She's trying to sort things out, Troy, as best she can."

"Good for her," he snarled. "You've got to tell me where she is, Evelyn—I've been offered a job in the States and I'd have to sell the house. I can't do that without at least consulting her."

"Fax me the details and I'll see she gets it right away."

"Thanks, but no, thanks—she's my *wife*, Evelyn!"

"If she hadn't been so insistent, I wouldn't have promised."

Insistent. Determined to stay away from him. To hide so he'd never find her. Too bad, Lucy, he thought grimly. This time it's not going to work. "If I'm to move from Vancouver, if I'm to divorce her, then I have to see her first. You surely must understand that." There, he had said it. He had actually used the word.

"Oh, Troy," Evelyn said faintly, "has it come to that?"

"I'm tired of being in limbo. Neither married nor free," he replied implacably.

"I do understand that your position's untenable." There was another of the long pauses that were quite out of character for Evelyn. Then she said slowly, "I believe Marcia's in touch with Lucy—you might try her... Oh, there's my doorbell—I'm going to a play with some friends. I've got to go, Troy."

Marcia was the eldest of Evelyn's three daughters. Marcia and Troy rarely saw eye to eye on anything. After saying goodbye to Evelyn, he dialed Marcia's number and made a huge effort to modulate his tone. "Marcia?

Troy here. I wondered if you would give me Lucy's address. Evelyn was busy when I called her.''

You lying bastard, he told himself. But it's all in a good cause.

One of Marcia's virtues, in Troy's opinion, was her supreme incuriosity about other people's lives. "She's staying on an island off the coast of Nova Scotia," Marcia said. "Let me think... Shag Island—that's it. Near Yarmouth. She's working at a guest house called the Seal Bay Inn. Sounds like the end of the world to me, but you know Lucy—she always was a bit off the wall.''

If Lucy hadn't decided on impulse to go sailing for four weeks in Tortola, he, Troy, would never have met her. "Thanks," he said and, not above pumping her, added, "Have you seen Lucy lately?''

"Goodness, no. You wouldn't catch me going on a smelly old fishing boat to some godforsaken island. Not my thing at all. She'll be home in a month or so; I'll see her then.''

"What took her there, do you know?''

"She got laid off at the bookstore where she was working. A friend of Cat's knows the couple who runs the inn—they needed someone for the summer, I guess.'' Marcia yawned. "The sort of harebrained scheme Lucy loves.''

Cat was Lucy's younger sister. "Well, thanks for the information, Marcia. Should you be talking to Lucy, you could forget we've had this conversation—okay?''

"Whatever you like," Marcia said indifferently. "If you were to take my advice, Troy, you'd cut your losses as far as Lucy's concerned.''

"I may just do that.''

"Well," she replied with patent surprise, "I'm very glad to hear it—I think she's behaved deplorably the last couple of years."

It was one thing for Troy to think that, another to hear Lucy's sister say so. "She lost her child, Marcia."

"So did you. But she's the one who's been running away from her responsibilities ever since."

He could feel his throat closing with the old pain, and in his heart of hearts he recognized the kernel of truth in Marcia's judgement. "Thanks for the address," he said huskily. "Don't work too hard." Very carefully Troy replaced the receiver in its cradle.

One of the many things which had distressed him unutterably in the last six months he and Lucy had lived together had been watching her withdraw from people, from her clients and her friends—she who had always delighted in the company of others. She was a certified massage therapist, and had worked one day a week after Michael was born to keep her hand in; after he had died she had lost all interest in her job.

In Ottawa she'd worked in a chain bookstore, an impersonal milieu that demanded nothing from her in the way of intimacy. And now she'd retreated still further, to spend the summer on an isolated island.

Shag Island. He'd get Vera to make a reservation under a false name at the Seal Bay Inn and this time next week he'd be face to face with Lucy. In the meantime he'd get in touch with the institute and tell them he needed a little more time to make his decision.

After that, whatever happened, he'd have to get on with his life.

CHAPTER TWO

As TROY strode down the long concrete wharf in his rubber boots, his canvas bag slung over one shoulder, the sea wind tugged at his hair; *Seawind* had been the name of the sloop he'd been skippering in the Virgin Islands when he'd first met Lucy.

A tangle of dried seaweed cracked under his boots. He glanced down, his nerves strung tight as catgut. He might look just like another tourist on holiday. But he wasn't a tourist. His only reason for being here was to go and see Lucy. Although this time not in an immaculate yacht. Unless he was mistaken, one of the workmanlike Cape Islanders clustered at the very end of the wharf was going to take him to his destination.

From the flat deck of a boat called *Four Angels* a man of about forty with a weathered face called, "You goin' to Shag Island?"

"That's right."

"Come on aboard, then. Hand yer gear down to Gus, and watch yer step."

Although Gus looked about fourteen, he swung Troy's heavy bag down on to the deck with agility. Troy climbed down the metal rungs set into the side of the wharf and felt the gunwale dip under his weight. *Four Angels* was even less prepossessing up close than she had been at a distance—her anchors rusty, her deck stained with the debris of years of fishing. But as Clarence, her skipper, introduced himself he gave Troy a broad smile, his blue eyes twinkling. Her engine started with a well-bred purr and she backed between two other boats into the open water with a precision Troy could appreciate.

There was another man sharing the deck with him, an elderly man with a crop of salt-white hair. Troy smiled at him and said, "My name's Troy Donovan. Are you staying at the Seal Bay Inn as well?"

"Hubert Woollner." A pair of eyes as fierce as a falcon's stared at him beneath bushy brows. "I own my own place on the south end of the island. Near the lighthouse."

"Come on, Hubert," Clarence interjected. "You own the whole darn island, from the lighthouse to the cliffs— tell the truth, now."

"Steer the boat, Clarence, and mind your own business."

Hubert had spoken without rancor. Clarence chuckled. "You are my business. The way fishin' is these days, it's a good thing I got this here ferry service to fall back on. Gotta feed the family somehow."

"The boat's named after Clarence's family," Hubert said to Troy. "A touch of poetic license."

"Named after the wife and me three daughters. Not that they're always angels. You married, Mr Donovan?"

"Yes," Troy said, and waited for someone to ask if Lucy Donovan was his wife.

But Clarence was following his own train of thought. "Then you know what I'm talkin' about. There's days I think I should've named her *Four Devils*. But there wouldn't be much luck callin' a boat that, now, would there? So *Four Angels* she is, and more power to her." With a flourish he spat over the gunwales and revved up the engine. The bow bit into the waves, the wake bubbled from the stern and the wharf fell back behind them.

For a moment Troy forgot about Lucy and the purpose of his visit in the sheer pleasure of being on the sea again; in the last year and a half he'd lost his enthusiasm for sailing. Then Hubert asked, "Did you come for the long-billed dowitcher?"

"The who?" said Troy.

"So you're not a birder?" Hubert said sternly.

"I know a duck from a pelican," Troy remarked, raising his voice over the roar of the engine and the hissing of the sea. He'd always been more interested in snorkeling and diving in the Caribbean than in the birds.

"Humph. So you wouldn't know what a shag is, then?"

A long ago crossword clue flickered through Troy's memory. "A fish like a herring," he hazarded.

"That's a shag. See that bird flying low over the water?" Obligingly Troy looked to starboard, seeing a black bird with a skinny neck flapping madly away from *Four Angels*. "That's a shag," Hubert went on. "It's the local name for a cormorant—in this case an immature double-crested cormorant. What made you come to Shag Island if you're not a birder?"

Amused by this inquisition, Troy prevaricated, "I needed a holiday. I work in a crowded hospital in a big city and a few days on an island sounded like heaven."

"If you're staying a few days, Keith'll fix you up with a pair of binoculars. Keith McManus owns the inn. Doesn't have much to say for himself, but he knows his birds."

This was clearly high praise. "Is it a one-man operation, then?" Troy asked with low cunning.

"Anna helps out—his wife. They've got a hired girl this summer as well." For a moment the fierce old eyes softened. "A real beauty, she is."

Spreading his feet on the deck and absently noticing that he'd never lost his sea-legs, Troy said, "And what's her name?"

"Lucy Barnes," said Hubert.

With another of the explosions of rage that seemed to haunt him these days Troy realized that no one had connected his name with Lucy's because Lucy was no longer using his name. She'd reverted to her maiden name. As if, he thought savagely, he, Troy, didn't exist. As though her marriage was better forgotten.

Hubert was still talking. "...myself if I was forty years younger. You'll meet her if you're staying for a while. She and Mrs Mossop take turns with the cooking."

Lucy had been the cook on *Seawind*. "Who else lives on the island?" Troy asked.

"Mrs Mossop—she's a widow. Myself. Quentin—he's an artist; he puts big globs of paint on a canvas and calls it *Untitled Composition* and the critics rave over it. This new-fangled stuff they call art; I can't give it the time of day."

Four Angels had rounded a headland and was headed due west. On the horizon lay a long island—the small pinnacle of a lighthouse at one end, cliffs rearing from the sea like the blunt head of a whale from the other. Filling his nostrils with clean salt air, Troy asked, "Is that Shag Island?"

"That's it."

"Not very many people for the size of the island."

"I keep the numbers low because of the petrels," Hubert said.

"Petrol?" Troy repeated, puzzled.

Hubert raised his brows heavenwards. "Petrels are birds. Leach's storm petrels nest on the southern end of the island. So I don't allow cats on the island and we use a dory to go from this boat to shore, to do away with the possibility of rats. There aren't any racoons or foxes to prey on them. Too many humans would be just as bad. I decided a long time ago that we're the most destructive species there is. So I won't let Keith expand the inn.''

"How do you keep the guests at the inn from doing any damage?''

"That's one of Lucy's jobs. I pay part of her salary.''

"So you're a benevolent despot?''

Hubert gave a cackle of laughter. "I've willed the island to a conservation society, with so many provisos and heretofores it'll take them forever to sort it out. But in the meantime the petrels'll be safe. And that's what counts.''

"Birds over people?'' Troy asked with conscious provocation.

"Birds and people coexisting,'' Hubert retorted with a gleam in his eye. "Non-interference. Respect for the intricacies of nature. I'll invite you for dinner one evening, providing you don't mind canned beans, and we'll thrash it out.''

"You're a proselytizer, Mr Woollner.''

"Hubert's the name. By the time you leave I'll make sure you know a least sandpiper from a semipalmated. How long did you say you were staying.''

"I didn't say...because I'm not sure.''

"You'll stay a while. The island gets you that way. Got me fifty years ago, and she's been like a mistress to me ever since.'' He pulled at his ear, laughter sparking his tawny old eyes. "Less trouble than a woman in the long run, I dare say.''

They both fell silent as the island drew closer, until Troy could see rocks girdled with kelp, ranks of spruce trees huddled and bent against the wind, and to the north the long sweep of a low-lying field, with drifts of yellow wildflowers between it and the shore. The Lucy he had fallen in love with would be very much at home on Shag Island.

With a kindling of excitement he wondered if during a summer spent in this wild and beautiful place she'd found herself again...become the old Lucy, the passionate, laughing creature who'd turned his life upside-down when he'd first met her five years ago. Maybe—just maybe—she'd welcome him with open arms, with all the delight in his presence that had always, paradoxically, both nourished and humbled him.

Clarence cut the engines and Gus went forward to hook the big pink buoy bobbing on the waves. Onshore a wooden dock sloped into the sea; a man was hauling a red-painted boat down it into the water. He clambered aboard, and in a swirl of wake headed for *Four Angels*.

"That's Keith," Hubert said. "You'll arrive at the inn nicely in time for dinner."

"Where's your house?" Troy asked idly.

"I took over one of the bungalows where the light-keepers used to live. Mrs Mossop lives in the other one. Here's Keith now—hand down the gear first, then get in and sit near the bow."

Refraining from saying that boats had been part of his life since he was a boy, Troy did as he was told and introduced himself to Keith. A considerable part of Keith's face was hidden by the twin growths of a fiery red beard and a mop of red hair; between them peered a pair of hazel eyes that were not so much unfriendly as desperately shy. Keith mumbled his name and with ill-disguised relief swiveled to face the motor.

When they reached the shore, he drove the boat right up on the slip. Troy stepped out and hauled it still further over the thick wood slats beneath which the salt water gurgled and slapped. He gave a hand to Hubert, who gathered up a small backpack, waved a cheery goodbye and set off along a trail that followed the curve of the shore.

"This way," Keith said, and without looking to see if Troy was following set off on another trail that led in the opposite direction through the woods.

The ground was springy and the air smelled sweetly of moss and fallen needles; Troy tramped along, his heart pounding in his chest because at any moment now he might see Lucy.

Tucked into a sheltered cove, the Seal Bay Inn was a two-storied cedar building, with an expanse of glass overlooking the ocean and a generous deck where chairs and pots of flowers were scattered; a small cabin sat a little apart from it in the trees. "It's delightful," Troy said spontaneously. "Who built it, Keith?"

"Me."

"You did a fine job."

Keith said nothing, merely gestured for Troy to go ahead of him through the sliding glass door. It opened into a spacious living area paneled in pine; the sea and sky were as much a part of the room as the comfortable sofas and well-furnished bookshelves. An alcove was taken up by a long trestle table laid for dinner. Then Troy heard footsteps coming down the hall and felt his heart rise into his throat. Lucy. It had to be Lucy.

But the woman who entered the room was very different from Lucy. For one thing, she was at least eight months pregnant; for another her hair was as straight and dark as Martine's, although it was pulled back into a ponytail from a face unadorned by make-up. She said in a friendly voice, "You're our new guest—Mr Daniels, I believe?"

Struggling to overcome a crushing disappointment, Troy remembered that he'd reserved under a false name to avoid alerting Lucy to his arrival. He said awkwardly, and untruthfully, "I hope you don't mind—my friend Daniels couldn't come at the last minute. So I took his place. Donovan's the name."

"That's no problem. Welcome to Shag Island, Mr Donovan. I'm Anna McManus."

Because her smile was innocent of guile, Troy felt ashamed of his deception. Fighting down the urge to ask about Lucy, he went upstairs with her and approved his room.

"Dinner's in half an hour—I ring the bell," she said. "The bar's downstairs; you keep your own tab. Please let me know if there's anything we can do to make your stay more pleasant."

Give me back my wife, he thought wildly, and with relief closed the door behind her. He'd hoped to meet Lucy with some semblance of privacy; now, it would seem, she'd be waiting on all the guests at the dinner table.

Her face, when she first saw him, would tell him all he needed to know. He must keep his eyes glued to her face.

But thirty-five minutes later, when Troy was seated in the alcove, the woman who carried in the bowls of steaming fish chowder was plump and middle-aged, her cheeks flushed from the heat of the stove. The widowed Mrs Mossop, thought Troy, and politely made conversation with the four other guests, whose names he'd forgotten as soon as he'd heard them and whose impassioned discussion about a buff-breasted sandpiper couldn't have interested him less. Lucy surely hadn't left the island, he thought, his throat constricting with terror. She must be in the kitchen, working behind the scenes. She had to be.

However, Anna was the cook that evening—so Mrs Mossop informed them, when one of the guests complimented her on the roast chicken. "It's Lucy's day off," she said. "She'll be back in the morning, and I wouldn't be surprised if she'll make blueberry pancakes for breakfast; she was going berry-picking today."

So she was here. He could relax.

But tomorrow seemed an aeon away. Troy ate his apple pie with less attention than it deserved, swallowed his coffee and excused himself. Hoping to bump into Lucy, he hiked along the shore until dusk. Then, knowing he hadn't got a hope of sleeping yet, because he was still jet-lagged, he sat in one of the chairs on the deck, watching the last peach flush fade from the sky.

His body merged with the shadows. A pale arm of the Milky Way gestured gracefully across the heavens, whose blackness was studded with larger, brighter stars, their cold, impersonal light making him all the lonelier.

An owl hooted in the distance. A crescent moon rose, curved like an empty bowl; the tide sucked at the rocks. And then, overriding the sounds of the sea, Troy heard the one voice he'd been wanting to hear for months. Lucy's voice. He twisted to face the woods and saw two people standing close together on the little porch of the cabin.

"Thanks so much, Quentin," Lucy was saying, her clear, light voice carrying through the velvet darkness. "I had a lovely day. I promise I'll make you some blueberry muffins tomorrow."

"I got you home later than I'd planned—you have to get up so early in the morning."

"It was worth it."

"I'll drop by tomorrow for the muffins."

"Great."

Because Troy's eyes were so well adjusted to the night, he had no trouble seeing Quentin lean forward, kiss Lucy, then move back. His fingernails digging into the chair, he missed Quentin's next, low-voiced remark; Lucy laughed lightheartedly in return and went inside the cabin. Quentin flipped on a flashlight and disappeared down the path. Lucy closed the door and almost immediately a soft light glowed through the windows facing the sea, as though she had lit a candle.

Troy surged to his feet. On the long plane flight from Vancouver he had played with a number of different scenarios for the meeting between him and Lucy; none of them had included another man. Every one of his carefully reasoned speeches vanishing from his mind, he jumped over the railing of the deck and marched across the grass. Raising his fist, he knocked on Lucy's door.

"Coming!" she called, and even as she opened the door was saying, "Did you forget——?"

Her voice broke off. Because the light was behind her, Troy couldn't see the expression on her face, although her gasp of shock and her instinctive step backward were only too obvious. Pushing past her, he went inside.

She had lit two oil lamps—one beside the double bed, one on the table by the window. It took him less than two seconds to see the marks of her occupancy in the tiny cabin, none of which included a photograph of either himself or Michael. Stationing himself against the edge of the table, he said viciously, "What a cozy little setup—does the artist go along with it?"

"*Troy*! What are *you* doing here?" Her face paled, and suddenly she stepped to meet him, her fingers digging into his wrist under his light wool sweater. "Mother— is she all right? There's nothing wrong, is there?"

"There's a great deal wrong, which has nothing to do with your mother or your sisters and everything to do with us."

"You frightened me..."

He glanced down. It was Lucy's left hand that was clasping his wrist. Her finger was bare of the narrow gold band he had given her on their wedding-day. He said roughly, "Where's your wedding-ring? And your engagement ring?"

She jerked her hand away. "I left the sapphire in Ottawa—a busy kitchen is no place for an expensive ring." Her gray eyes openly defiant, she added, "I took off my wedding-band before I got on the boat to come over here."

"You left your married name behind as well. Isn't Donovan good enough for you any more?"

Suspicion had darkened her eyes. Ignoring his question, she said, "It was a Mr Daniels who was supposed to arrive today. Not you."

"I made the reservation under a false name," Troy said.

She was standing so close to him that her scent drifted to his nostrils. As though this was the only cue his body needed, it sprang to life, desire shooting sparks amid his anger like fresh wood tossed on to a fire. She looked wonderful, and this, too, fueled his rage. Her bare legs and her face were lightly tanned, her full breasts pushed at her loose cotton sweater, and her hair, longer than he had ever seen it, was a thick mass of mahogany curls. When Troy had last seen her, five months ago in Ottawa, she'd been thin and pale, with hollows under her cheekbones.

The last vestige of speech, planned or otherwise, vanished from Troy's brain. He put his arms around Lucy, pulled her against the length of his body and kissed her.

She fit. He knew her as he knew himself. She was his.

His kiss deepened, his hands rediscovering with frantic hunger the arch of her ribs, the little bump of her vertebrae where her neck met her shoulders, the labyrinth of her soft, fragrant hair. I've come home, he thought, his rage dropping away like a garment no longer needed.

He had felt the shock slam through Lucy's frame when he had first touched her; she had been standing as rigid as an iron bar in his embrace. But then she began to tremble and shake, like aspen leaves in the wind, clutching his sweater as if she might fall down were she to let go. Troy parted her lips with his tongue, wanting to savor the sweetness of her mouth, aching for her to open to him like a sunflower to the golden light of morning, to bend to his touch like long grass to a summer breeze.

"Lucy," he whispered, showering kisses on her lips, her cheeks, her throat. "Lucy, I love you so much." And somewhere, distantly, he remembered that these words had never been part of his plan.

She shoved against his chest with a strength that jarred every nerve in his body, and wrenched her mouth free. "Let go!" she cried. "Troy, let go of me or I'll scream the place down."

She looked entirely capable of doing so. Trying to gather his wits, which were scattered like confetti at a wedding, Troy said urgently, "You felt it, too, Lucy—you must have. It was like coming home after a long absence to the one you never meant to leave. It couldn't only have been me who felt that way—tell me it wasn't!''

"I don't want to go home!'' she cried, in a voice raw with pain. "Why do you think I left in the first place? Because I couldn't bear it—because it was killing me.''

"Say it, why don't you?'' he rasped. "Because I was killing you—that's what you mean, isn't it?''

Behind the question lay all the pain of their last six months together. Because if Lucy had withdrawn from her clients and her friends, she had also withdrawn from Troy, in a way that had devastated him.

In the first few days after the baby had died Lucy hadn't cried at all. Stunned, blank-faced, she had wandered around the house like a lost soul. Then one day a neighbor who had been away had innocently asked after him and Lucy had broken down, shutting herself in the nursery and sobbing for hours at a time. Although Troy had done his best to comfort her, he had been fatally hampered by the rawness of his own grief, and, without him being quite sure how it had happened, her withdrawal had become a pattern that he'd never been able to break.

Worst than that, though, had been Lucy's refusal to make love with him—her almost hysterical repudiation of the intimacy that had bound them together. At first Troy had understood. Even though he had been struggling, for her sake, to keep his own emotions under control, for days at a time, and from moment to moment, he had lived on the very edge of falling apart; and he had sensed the same fragility in Lucy. But later, when he had gone to her for consolation, desperate for a physical closeness that might keep the blackness of his sorrow at bay, she had struck him away.

She was afraid of getting pregnant again, or so she had said; she couldn't bear to start another baby. It had made sense, and Troy had believed her. However, as week after week had passed, and she'd continued, stony-faced, to reject him, Troy had begun to doubt the rapture they had once shared, and even the love that bound them together; the woman who was his wife had become a woman he no longer knew. And that had been the cruelest cut of all. Lucy, his beloved wife, had turned into a stranger.

Shaking his head like a wounded animal, Troy came back to the present. Lucy had stepped away from him, perhaps frightened by something in his face, her body rigid with tension. She said, "I stayed away just so we wouldn't go on hurting each other like this."

"You're a coward, Lucy."

She flinched. Then, raising her chin, she said, "Maybe instead I know when to let go."

It was Troy's turn to flinch. His naïve assumption that he might have fallen out of love with Lucy had vanished without a trace at the very first sight of her; if anything he loved her all the more. That he had even considered the possibility of his love being dead seemed laughable in the unalterable fact of her presence. Let go of her? He couldn't. He wouldn't.

He might have to. She had taken off his ring and was no longer using his name. She had pushed him away when he'd kissed her. She had—to use her own words—let him go.

Then she said, and there could be no mistaking her sincerity, "Troy, I don't want to cause you more pain. Can't we start this conversation over again?" She swallowed, the small movements of her throat filling him with frenzied longing. "Where did you come from? And why did you come?"

The table was hard against the backs of his thighs. Troy wrapped his fingers around the curved wood to keep himself from touching her and said harshly, "I came from Vancouver, which is where I happen to live—remember?"

Because the door to the cabin was still open a fraction, small brown moths were fluttering at the threshold. Lucy went to close the door, then leaned against it, visibly needing its support. "Why are you so angry?"

She had kissed Quentin, and laughed with him in the intimate darkness in front of her cabin. But Troy she had pushed away. "Oh, I'm not angry," Troy said sarcastically. "I just love seeing you with another man—promising to make him muffins, for Pete's sake—when for the last four months you haven't even done me the courtesy of a phone call to let me know where you are."

"We're separated," she said mutinously, pushing her hands in the pockets of her blue shorts.

He looked at her in silence. Her face was almost as well known to him as his own. Her cheeks were flushed, her features given character by the imperious bump in her nose and by her brows, dark as the wings of a bird. Her eyes were, like his own, gray, although in certain lights they swam mysteriously into depths of blue. "Separation must agree with you," he said deliberately. "You look better than you have since Michael died."

"*Don't!*" she said in a choked voice.

Troy fought for control, bunching his knuckles against the table. But for far too long his feelings had been cooped up inside him, and the sight of her—so beautiful, so sorely missed, so unattainable—was more than he could stand.

"Don't, what? Don't mention Michael's name?" he flared. "Pretend he never existed? We both know better than that, Lucy. We know his death was the reason you moved out on me." Not for the life of him could he have disguised the anguish in his voice as he added, "You don't even have a photo of him here... Do you hate him so much for dying?"

"I loved him too much to ever hate him for anything," she whispered. "I'm trying to forget what happened——"

"Forget *Michael*?"

"I'm trying to accept his death, to move on—that's why I keep my photos of him out of sight."

"Move on with Quentin? Is that the plan? How clever of you to have taken off your wedding-ring before you got here."

"Troy, you can't push your way in here and start throwing accusations at me. Nothing gives you that right!"

"I do happen to be your husband," he said, with deadly calm. "Or are you trying to forget that, too?"

"How can I? You won't let me!"

He took a deep breath. "You asked why I came here. I came to offer you a choice. Either we live together as husband and wife or I want a divorce."

Her eyes widened and her whole body tensed, like a sparrow who, safe in its hedgerow, had suddenly sighted a hawk perched on a nearby branch. She stared at him blankly while the slow seconds ticked by, and for the life of him Troy couldn't have guessed what she was thinking. Then she said, her voice not quite steady, "That sounds more like an ultimatum than a choice."

"You can call it what you like. I've gone on long enough being neither one thing nor the other—I'm not married because you refuse to live with me, but I'm not divorced either, so I'm not free to pursue any other options."

"Other women, you mean," she flashed.

"I didn't say that, Lucy." Belatedly Troy struggled to find the right words. "I want intimacy and companionship and a family—all the things you and I shared that felt so right. The things that made me so happy. I still want them with you, of course I do. But——"

"I can't, Troy! Not again, never again . . . It hurts too much."

It was a cry from the heart. "You can't hide forever," he said fiercely. "You never were afraid of living, Lucy. When I met you, you had enormous courage."

"That was then. This is now. I've changed; you've got to accept that."

"I won't allow you to turn into someone less than who you are!"

"Maybe you have no control over it," she retorted. "I'm not one of your patients—I'm not a nurse you can order around."

"Dammit, I'm not like that! I love you—that's why I'm here."

"Love should set you free," she said incoherently. "You brandish love in front of me like a set of chains."

With deadly emphasis Troy said, "So the answer's divorce."

"Stop putting words into my mouth! I've seen you once in the last year, yet you waltz in here, as though you own the place, and expect me to make a huge decision with all kinds of ramifications in the space of five minutes, just because it's convenient for you—you really do have a nerve, Troy."

"So how long will it take you to make up your mind?"

"How can I possibly know that?" she snapped.

"You want to have your cake and eat it too," he said furiously. "Keep me dangling like some kind of tame rabbit and in the meantime live exactly as you please. It won't wash, Lucy. I'm sick to death of it."

"I'm not making a decision at eleven o'clock at night that's going to affect my whole life," she seethed. "Go home, Troy. On the first plane. I'll write to you; I promise."

Knowing he was shooting himself in the foot, yet hearing the words spill from his mouth, Troy sneered, "And does that promise mean any more to you than the blueberry muffins you promised Quentin?"

"You really are intolerable," Lucy cried. "Get out of here. I've had more than enough and right now divorce seems like a very viable option." She whirled and flung the door open. "I've said I'll write to you, and I will."

He let go of the table, flexing his fingers, and crossed the painted wooden floorboards. "You can't fool me— you don't like the word divorce any more than I do. You might want to think about that tomorrow while you're mixing that batch of muffins." He looked straight into her eyes. "You might also want to think of what best honors our son's memory. Running away from reality like a child afraid of the dark—or embracing everything that life brings with it, both good and bad, happy and tragic." Lightly he ran one finger down her cheek to the corner of her mouth. "Goodnight."

He walked out on to the porch and closed the door in Lucy's face. Her jaw had dropped at his last speech— almost the only one he'd made that he'd rehearsed beforehand—and she'd been, temporarily anyway, speechless. He had needed that small victory, because his whole body felt sore, as though an unseen opponent had pummeled him mercilessly against a concrete wall.

She hadn't agreed to a divorce. But she had accused him of holding her captive with a love that was like chains.

An image he hated with all his soul.

CHAPTER THREE

WHEN the bell chimed for breakfast the next morning, Troy had just finished shaving. He gazed at himself in the mirror, dabbing at the small cut on his chin. He looked exactly like a man who'd had about three hours' sleep. Although three was probably an exaggeration.

His eyes, deepset at the best of times, were now bruised by the remnants of a night trapped between nightmares and the raging hunger of his sexuality. To know that Lucy was so near and yet so far had been torture. Worse, perhaps, had been the extinguishing of any hope that he no longer cared for her. He loved her—heart, soul and body. He'd probably, he thought gloomily, running a comb through his hair, love her forever.

For all the good it would do him.

His mother had once compared the color of his eyes to the rock from the quarry near where he'd grown up. Maybe chains were that same unrevealing, stony gray. If he stayed here, would he be treating Lucy like some medieval prisoner? Manacling her to him by force?

His cut appeared to have stopped bleeding; he should go down to breakfast. He straightened the mirror, remembering how Lucy had used to love tracing the strong line of his nose and the curve of his lips down to the cleft in his chin with her fingertip. She had used to find him irresistible.

Not any more.

If he were smart he'd take her advice and get on the first flight out of here. And then he'd accept the job in

Arizona. If she did come back to him they could live just as well in Arizona as in Vancouver; with her at his side, he didn't care where he lived.

She was afraid of love. Afraid of its costs and penalties.

Or else she hated his guts; that didn't seem too unlikely either.

He adjusted the collar of his blue open-necked shirt and then, as though he couldn't help himself, he replaced his wedding-ring on his left hand.

When he went downstairs only his place was empty at the trestle table; the birders had all been up at dawn and were now ravenously tucking into heaped blueberry pancakes and jugs of hot maple syrup. The buff-breasted sandpiper had been usurped by the long-billed dowitcher as the main topic of discussion. Troy drained his orange juice and helped himself to a pancake.

"Would you like coffee?"

His fork clattered to the floor. He bent to pick it up and said, without looking at Lucy, "Thanks."

She leaned forward to reach his mug. She was wearing a print skirt with a crisp white blouse, and in profile looked cool and unapproachable. Suddenly hating her for her composure, he said loudly, "Lucy, you haven't kissed me good morning."

As if he'd uttered an obscenity, every one of the birders was staring at him. "Why would she do that?" the bald one blurted.

"She's my wife," Troy announced with a bland smile. "Who else would she kiss good morning?"

For a wild moment he thought Lucy was going to dump the coffee-pot and its contents over his head.

Openly laughing at her, feeling more alive than he had for weeks, he said, "Don't do it, sweetheart."

With a gasp of pure outrage Lucy straightened to her full height. "We're separated," she said, her gaze sweeping to include every occupant of the table but Troy. "We're going to get a divorce."

Troy pushed back his chair and stood up. "So is that your decision?"

Her eyes blazed into his. "Yes."

"Ah . . . In that case you won't mind if I hang around for a few days. Obviously, if you're going to divorce me, you don't love me any more. So my presence shouldn't matter to you one way or the other."

"You ought to be down on your knees giving thanks that this is a coffee-pot and not a carving knife," she grated. "Stop being insufferable, Troy, and go back to Vancouver."

"I think not," he said lazily. "You know, you say you want a divorce, but you really don't look indifferent to me, Lucy, my love."

"*Oh!*" she gasped, turned on her heel and scurried down the hall.

Troy said, with an innocent smile, sitting down again and picking up his knife and fork, "These pancakes are wonderful, aren't they? Is it any wonder that I married her?"

The bearded birder said determinedly, "Neville, are you sure it was an alder flycatcher in that spruce tree?"

"Heard it," Neville said succinctly.

"There are several leasts near the lighthouse."

"That's where I saw the sharp-tailed sparrow," the bald man offered.

Troy ate his pancakes. Maybe he'd go in search of Hubert this morning. If he was going to stay here for a few days he should probably learn what a dowitcher looked like.

He'd let Lucy stew for the day. At least he'd given her something to think about.

He took his coffee out on the deck. Three brown ducks were bobbing about in the seaweed, while little rustlings and chirps came from the shrubs around the inn. Otherwise the only sounds were the soft rise and fall of the waves. It was very peaceful, and perhaps it was this that brought Troy to his senses. While the scene at breakfast had given him considerable pleasure, it had been less than wise. What the devil was he trying to do? Push Lucy into a divorce?

The morning sun shivered on the water. I'm fighting for my life, Troy thought soberly. That's why I've come here. But I've got to try and keep my feelings in check and use my head—or I'll blow it.

A boy of perhaps eight or nine bounced up the steps from the shore, stopped in his tracks when he saw Troy sitting there and said eagerly, "Did you see it? The Cape May warbler?"

There were binoculars strung around the boy's neck and spruce needles caught in his hair; his legs, bared by denim shorts, were crisscrossed by long red scratches. "No," said Troy. "I don't know much about birds."

"You *don't*? Why'd you come here, then?"

"I came to see Lucy...she's my wife."

"Yeah?" Suspicion darkened the boy's hazel eyes; his face was thin and vital under a crop of straight brown hair. "She never told us about you."

Troy had suspected as much. Smothering his hurt, and knowing that for some reason it was important to tell the boy the truth, he said, "We haven't lived together for over a year. But we're still married."

"Oh. Did you have a fight?"

"A big one," Troy said wryly.

"When my mum and me have a fight, she always says we should make up before the sun goes down."

"I think your mum's on to something there. Are you Anna and Keith's son?"

"Yep." The boy scowled. "My mum's going to have a baby."

"I know. Don't you like the idea?"

"A baby'll cry all the time. Lucy doesn't like it, either. When she got here and found out my mum was pregnant, she nearly went home again."

But she hadn't left, Troy thought with a flash of hope. She'd stayed here instead. "My name's Troy," he said. "What's yours?"

"Stephen. I hate being called Steve."

"Then I won't call you that. Would you like to show me some of the birds here, Stephen?"

"Sure! I gotta have breakfast first, but I'll be out in ten minutes, okay?"

His sneakers thudded across the deck and he disappeared indoors. Glad to be alone, for his eyes were suddenly glazed with tears, Troy gazed out to sea. Would Michael, had he lived, have grown up to be so engaging and so full of energy?

He'd never know the answer to that question.

Restlessly he went upstairs, changed into old clothes and brushed his teeth. He was waiting on the deck when Stephen charged out of the door; the boy was waving an extra pair of binoculars and a bird book. "I was gonna go and see Hubert," he said. "D'you know him?"

"We met on the boat."

"Hubert knows where there's a long-billed dowitcher—that's a real rare bird."

So he was finally to meet the long-billed dowitcher, Troy thought, with an inner twinge of amusement. And

Hubert would no doubt be impressed to see him armed with a pair of binoculars. "Let's go," he said.

People interested in birds, Troy soon learned, traveled at a snail's pace.

First Stephen got him to focus above a clump of goldenrod, and into the field of his binoculars leaped a small bird the same brilliant yellow as the flowers, shining like a jewel in the sun. Then he was introduced to another warbler, bedecked in orange, black and white, and to a plump rust-colored fox sparrow. By the time they finally arrived at Hubert's bungalow, Troy was getting a glimmering of why Neville and his crew had to be up at dawn every day.

As Hubert clumped down his steps Stephen said, "Troy's coming with us. He's married to Lucy."

The smile vanished from Hubert's face. "Is that true?" he barked.

Troy nodded. "Yes—although we've lived apart for the last year. I should have told you on the boat, Hubert. But I wasn't sure how she was going to react."

Hubert swept this aside. "She's got no money—you too tight to support her?"

Troy's eyes narrowed. "She wouldn't take my money," he said, and made no attempt to hide the confusion of emotions that this had caused him.

"Humph. She's a fine woman—why'd you split up?"

His own eyes as unrelenting as Hubert's, Troy said, "Because our infant son died. Crib death. No reason, no sense, no warning. What else would you like to know?"

Hubert said gruffly, "Sorry, old man. Should learn to mind my own business."

Stephen piped, "Is that why Lucy doesn't want my mum to have a baby?"

"I expect so, Stephen. She was very sad when Michael died."

"Let's go see the dowitcher," Hubert said.

For the next three hours Troy was hauled through raspberry canes and alders and bogs; birding was not a hobby for weaklings.

He enjoyed himself far more than he had expected, although the long-billed dowitcher, a bird of indeterminate color that poked holes in the mud flats and seemed indistinguishable from its short-billed cousin, didn't seem worth all the fuss. But when Hubert said, "Meet me here at eleven tonight and I'll show you the petrels," Troy was happy to agree.

He went back to the inn, slept the afternoon away, and was able to contribute his two cents' worth to the dinner conversation. The meal, not to his surprise, was served by Mrs Mossop.

But at five to eleven, when his flashlight lit up Hubert's front steps, Hubert was not alone. The beam of another flashlight caught Troy full in the face and Lucy said crossly, "Hubert, you didn't tell me Troy was coming."

"Must've forgotten," Hubert said. "Let's go."

"You don't need me if Troy's going with you."

"I'm paying you to look after the petrels. Quit your bellyaching and come along."

Hubert set off behind the bungalows, where the light-house swept its cold blue light in an endless, repetitive circle. Lucy hunched her shoulders under her dark sweater and followed, and Troy brought up the rear. Unless he was mistaken, he had an ally in Hubert. Although Hubert's bulldozer tactics might do more harm than good.

Lucy was wearing faded, tight-fitting jeans; her long legs moved with an economical grace that did nothing for Troy's equanimity. They entered the woods, taking a narrow trail that wound through the spruce trees. Tall ferns brushed Troy's knees; the cool night air was fragrant with bayberry and damp moss.

Then Hubert stopped so suddenly that Lucy bumped into him. Troy caught at her from behind, steadying her, and felt the supple twist of her waist under his palms. Her hair tickled his nose. "Let go—I'm fine," she muttered, butting at him with her elbow.

"Shush," said Hubert, clicking off his light. "Hear 'em?"

Troy had totally forgotten the reason for the outing. He stood still, and from his left heard a plaintive series of whickers. But, instead of coming from the trees, the sound was underfoot. Another call rippled through the darkness, higher pitched, then another, still louder, until the woods were alive with the eerie, disembodied cries. He put a hand on Lucy's shoulder. "Is it the petrels? Where are they?"

"They have burrows underground. You're hearing the chicks; it's a hunger call." She pivoted. "See that?"

A black shape had whipped between the trees. "That's one of the adults," she breathed. "They stay out at sea for two or three days, feeding, then come in to feed the chick and relieve the other adult."

The pale glimmer of her face was lit with excitement. It was the old Lucy, Troy thought with a catch at his heart; it was months since he had seen her so animated, so caught up in anything but her own grief.

Hubert said bluffly, "I'm going to check on the owl's nest—you two stay here and wait for me. Then I'm going home by the other trail."

The beam of his flashlight flittered through the trees and was gone. Lucy said irritably, "As a matchmaker, he's got the subtlety of a bludgeon. What did you tell him about us, Troy?''

"I told him the truth," Troy said mildly. "How do the birds find their nests in the dark?"

He was genuinely interested in the answer; although he was more interested in keeping Lucy at his side in the intimate blackness of the night. She said grudgingly, "No one really knows. A sense of smell may be part of it...hear that? It's an adult on the ground, trying to find its burrow."

Her light picked out a small dark bird with elegant pointed wings, blundering around the forest floor. "I won't pick it up," she said softly. "They're beautiful to look at, but if you handle them too much they're apt to regurgitate a really stinky oil all over you. It's the way they bring food for the chicks."

Feeling his way, Troy said slowly, "They mean something to you."

She flicked off the light, as if she didn't want him to see her face. "They live nine months of the year on the open ocean, never touching land at all, and then they dig burrows in the depths of the forest to raise their young. I think they're amazing—they fascinate me."

"Do they come back to the same burrow year after year?"

She said reluctantly, "If they were successful in raising their chick, they will."

"The same pair of birds?"

Even more reluctantly she said, "Yes. Hubert banded one pair that's been together for fifteen years. I was here in June, when the adults were just starting to arrive. They haven't seen each other for the whole winter, and then they meet at the burrow. They make a kind of purring sound—a duet—as if they're happy to see one another."

Terrified of scaring her off, Troy said with a thread of laughter in his voice, "If I were a petrel, I guess I'd be purring right now. Thanks for telling me that."

Lucy looked up at him, her face very serious. "But we weren't successful in raising our young, were we?" she said. "So I—I think it's time you found a new mate."

"I don't want anyone else but you."

"I'm no good for you," she said raggedly. "I won't make love to you, Troy; that hasn't changed. I never want to have another child."

"There's no reason in the world why we should lose a second baby," Troy said, with all the conviction he could muster.

"There's no point in even talking about it." Unexpectedly she reached up, resting her hands on his shoulders; her lashes lowered at the shudder of pleasure he could in no way have controlled, and which she must have felt. "Please," she said, staring fixedly at his chest, "please believe me when I tell you the best thing you can do for yourself is leave here and forget me and find someone else."

Troy's heart was pounding in sick, heavy strokes. "Don't you love me any more?" he asked.

"I...I—no, I don't."

"Look at me and say that, Lucy," he demanded, capturing one of her hands in his and bringing it to his lips. Her fingertips were cool against his mouth.

She tried to jerk her hand free. "You've got to believe me!"

"You're forgetting that I probably know you better than anyone else in the world," Troy said forcefully. "You're honest and faithful and true. You told me five years ago you'd love me forever. I believed you then and I still do."

"How could I possibly have known when I married you what would happen? Other people's children die—never your own. If you'd said to me five years ago that four years later I—I wouldn't be able to bear to have you touch me, I'd have said you were out of your mind. But I was young and ignorant, and I thought I had the world by the tail. How could I have known what was going to happen?"

"Neither of us could have known. And it happened, Lucy. It happened. But life does go on, and we have to go on with it. Or else we might as well be dead ourselves."

Unconsciously she was clasping Troy's hand with all her strength, her oval nails marking his flesh. "I don't know how to make you understand!"

"I love you," he said strongly. "I'll always love you. Come back with me, Lucy, and let's give ourselves a second chance."

"No—no, I can't. I couldn't possibly do that."

Troy let out his breath in a harsh sigh, fighting the almost overwhelming need to take her in his arms. That morning he'd been convinced that if he was to win her back he had to keep his head. Follow your own advice, Troy, he told himself.

"Don't you remember what it was like after he died?" he said. "How we tiptoed around each other, being so polite, so careful of each other's feelings? We're not doing that any more, Lucy—that must be as obvious to you as it is to me. I've been here less than thirty-six hours and already we've had a couple of yelling matches and kissed each other until I, at least, was awake all night with wanting you. And we've talked more honestly to each other than we ever did then. I don't believe we can stand still—it's against nature."

"I won't come back to you," she repeated in a dead voice.

Over the constant chatter of the petrels Troy heard a twig snap, then saw the beam of Hubert's flashlight lance through the trees. "I'm going to do my best to change your mind," he said.

Lucy tugged her hand free. "Don't make me hate you," she cried.

"That's hardly my aim!"

"Saw both fledgelings," Hubert announced, puffing to catch his breath. "I'll take you to the nest next time we're out, Troy. Better still, Lucy can. I'm getting too old to be crashing around the woods after dark."

"Don't push your luck, Hubert," Lucy said. "I can always quit."

"You're as crazy about these goldarned birds as I am—don't talk to me about quitting. Ready to go, Troy?"

"Yeah. Stephen plans to take me out at some ungodly hour in the morning, so I'd better get some sleep."

"That's a fine young fellow," Hubert said. "Makes me wish I'd had a son of my own."

Lucy stamped her foot. "The next time I'm at your place I'm going to open the dictionary to the word 'tact' and make you memorize it, Hubert."

"Sooner or later all my friends tell me the same thing. Got so I count on it." Hubert's grin revealed uneven, yellowing teeth. "Too old to change."

"You're never too old to change," Lucy retorted.

"Darling Lucy, I've been trying to persuade you of that ever since I got here," Troy said.

"Troy Donovan, you make me so angry I could spit!"

"Glad to hear it," Troy said drily. "I'm going to bed. You coming?"

She said pungently, "Not in the way you mean. Goodnight, Hubert."

She set off down the narrow path at a breakneck clip. Troy said, "Thanks, Hubert, that was great," and jogged after her.

"You get her to show you the owl's nest," Hubert bellowed. "Got to be at night, though."

Sure, Troy thought, and finally caught up with Lucy. She was dodging tree roots and skirting rocks with an agility he had to admire; almost as much as he admired the way her bottom swung from side to side. He said breathlessly, nearly tripping over a fallen branch and saving himself by grabbing the nearest tree trunk, "Either you've put on weight or your jeans have shrunk."

She stopped in her tracks. "Why don't you go ahead of me?" she said between gritted teeth. "That way you might manage not to fall flat on your face."

"I'd rather concentrate on you."

"If Hubert's a bludgeon, then you're a battl-ax!"

"Go ahead, Lucy," Troy said kindly, "get it all off your chest." He eyed her breasts, which were rising and falling from a combination of exercise and emotion. "Too bad your sweater didn't shrink, too."

"You're behaving like a fourteen-year-old."

"Sexual deprivation does that to me."

Her hands on her hips, the flashlight shining on the scuffed toes of her sneakers, she said with sudden intensity, "You must have slept with someone in the last twelve months."

Balancing lightly on the balls of his feet, he answered, "Let me tell you a story. About ten days ago I dated one of the doctors at the hospital. Our third date. She let it be known that I'd be welcome in her bed, and with every intention of ending up there I went to her apartment with her... Do you know what happened?''

"I couldn't possibly guess," Lucy said coldly.

"She wasn't you." Troy gave an unamused bark of laughter. "Wrong size, wrong shape, wrong everything. I couldn't have made love with her to save my soul. So I left her apartment as if a rabid dog was at my heels and the next day I got your address from Marcia. Your mother, you'll be pleased to know, wouldn't give it to me."

"So you've never been unfaithful to me?" Lucy said in a strained voice.

"Never. I was a fool to even try; I see that now."

"You make it worse and worse," she cried.

With deliberate crudity, he demanded, "Would you rather I'd laid every nurse from Men's Surgical to Obstetrics?"

"No! Yes... Oh, God, I don't know."

Her face was anguished. Ruthlessly Troy pushed his advantage. "I'm sure you know the words in the old marriage vows—the ones that aren't fashionable any more. 'With my body I thee worship'. That's how I feel about you, Lucy. It's that simple."

Incredibly, a faint smile lifted the corners of her mouth. "Nothing's simple. If there's one thing I've learned the last few months, it's that."

He held his breath, praying she'd go on.

"Troy," she said quietly, "you're a good man—don't think I've lost sight of that. But I can't give you what you need and deserve. For your own sake leave here, and—and divorce me and start over. It would be best— believe me."

"No," he said.

Lucy closed her eyes, her shoulders slumped. "Then if you get hurt by staying here, I won't take responsibility for it."

"I'll look after myself," he said flatly. "I've had lots of practice in the last few months."

Her eyes flew open. "I really hate this," she whispered. "If you loved me at all, you'd leave."

"I'm staying," Troy said inflexibly, and felt the tension vibrating through every nerve in his body. Was he forcing her to a decision she wasn't ready to make? In which case he was doing more damage than good, driving her away when he meant to draw her close, hurting her again—she who had been hurt more than enough.

Or was he deceiving himself? Wilfully ignoring the unpalatable truth that Lucy no longer loved him? She didn't want him in her bed, nor would she give their marriage a second chance; she'd made that clear enough.

In which case he was the one who'd get hurt if he stayed. Just as she'd said.

But as the words "I'll leave tomorrow" formed themselves on Troy's tongue, Lucy said, "I'm exhausted, and I've got to get up early tomorrow—I'm going back." She started along the trail, not looking to see if he was following her.

Troy let her get ahead of him before he switched on his own flashlight and started picking his way through the trees. Indecision dogged his steps the whole way back to the inn, and that night confusion and self-doubt were his only bedfellows.

CHAPTER FOUR

AT DAWN the next morning Stephen introduced Troy to the intricacies of the flycatchers—all of which were small gray birds—and the charm of the chickadees and kinglets that foraged near the inn. Mrs Mossop served French toast and crisp bacon and piping hot coffee for breakfast; Lucy was nowhere to be seen.

Troy wasn't sorry. He'd said nothing to Anna about leaving, if only because he was no nearer a decision that morning than he had been the night before. He felt drained of energy, in no mood to face Lucy. After breakfast Stephen reappeared, with two packages of sandwiches, fruit and juice. "Want to go to the beach on the other side of the island?" he asked. "You gotta learn about sandpipers."

Sandpipers couldn't be as confusing as his own thoughts, Troy decided, and dredged up a smile. "Let's go."

The sun beat down from a cloudless sky. Stephen was as oblivious to the weather as he was to the brambles that scratched his bare legs; he chattered on about the school he went to on the mainland in the winter and how his father had taught him about birds as soon as he was big enough to hold binoculars. "I'm going to be a naturalist and study biology," he said. "Oh, look, there's a hummingbird—there's only one kind here, the ruby-throated."

It was hovering over a patch of wild mustard, its feathers glittering like the jewel for which it was named.

61

There had been hummingbirds at Troy's villa on Virgin Gorda the first time he had taken Lucy there; the first time they had made love, he thought numbly, and watched the hummingbird dart away.

"You okay?" Stephen asked.

"Hubert and Lucy and I went to see the petrels last night; I'm tired," Troy temporized, wishing Stephen's keenness of sight was restricted to birds.

Stephen said accusingly, "Lucy was crying when she was mixing the eggs this morning. Did you make her cry?"

Troy grimaced. "I don't know, Stephen. I guess she doesn't want me here."

Stephen screwed his face in thought. "I really like Lucy, and I like you, too—I don't see why you have to fight. Grownups are pretty weird sometimes."

"Ain't that the truth," Troy said wryly. "Where are these famous sandpipers?"

The beach was alive with them, and sorting them out distracted Troy from his troubles. He found them unexpectedly beautiful, with their scaled backs and clockwork movements; when they took flight, the flocks wheeling and turning, their bellies flashed white in the sun.

"Some of them fly eight thousand miles when they migrate," Stephen said. "They're storing up food right now for the journey."

That these tiny creatures could travel such immense distances somehow heartened Troy, and by the time he and Stephen returned to the lodge late in the afternoon, hot, sweaty and dirty, he was more at peace with himself. Stephen disappeared to do his chores. Troy changed into swim trunks and headed for the little beach north of the inn.

The water was like ice, which was no doubt why he had the beach to himself. After he'd swum several lengths back and forth, as fast as if he were in a race, he amused himself diving for rocks on the bottom. Then, shaking the water out of his ears, he waded back to shore and scrubbed dry with his towel.

His skin was tingling; considering that he'd had almost no sleep the last two nights, he felt astonishingly wide awake. He picked up a flat rock, skimming it over the surface of the water with an expertise he'd never lost and wondering if Stephen knew how to do that.

He'd have to teach him. He liked Stephen. Liked him a lot.

Something moved at the edge of Troy's vision. He looked around. With the familiar thump in his chest he saw Lucy step out into the clearing above the beach; she was wearing brief orange shorts and a green tank top. "Hello," he said.

"I didn't know you were here," she answered, scowling at him. "I sometimes come here to cool off before dinner—the kitchen gets pretty hot and it gives me a break."

She didn't want him here. On the beach. On the island. In her life. That much had been obvious last night and was even more obvious right now. "I'll leave you to it—I was just going." He picked up his towel and pushed his feet into his sneakers.

As he came closer Lucy crossed her arms tight over her chest; the breeze played with her hair, wafting it over her face. Her lips were set and she was studiously staring at the horizon. But as he came level with her her eyes skidded over his body as though of their own accord. Abruptly she reached out one hand. "Troy! What happened there?"

He glanced down. A long red scar, ugly and jagged, marred the left side of his ribcage. He said, "I fell. Skiing at Whistler, last February."

"You fell? But you never fall."

"A couple of beginners had strayed on to the slope. It was a choice of hitting one of them or wrapping myself around the nearest tree. The tree won."

In a shocked whisper she said, "You ski so fast—you could have been killed."

"I wouldn't be here bothering you if I had been, would I?"

"How can you say such a thing? I never wanted you dead!"

"No—you just don't want me," Troy said, with a depth of bitterness that had been months in the making.

"That's not—it's not that simple."

As if she couldn't help herself, she laid her palm over the scar; she must have felt the heavy pounding of his heart, because with an inarticulate sound that Troy couldn't possibly have categorized she suddenly rested her cheek on his cold, bare chest.

Her tank top was brief, clinging to her breasts, her cleavage an enticing shadow. Her legs seemed to go on forever. Clutching his towel in one hand, lifting her face with the other, Troy leaned forward and kissed her hard on the mouth. Her lips were warm and soft; against every instinct in his body he kept his kiss brief, not giving her the time either to resist him or reject him.

When he raised his head her eyes were a turbulent gray-blue, full of confusion. He wanted to tell her he loved her; he wanted to kiss her until she melted in his arms; he wanted to carry her to his bed and make love to her, and to hell with the consequences. He said,

"Enjoy your break," and walked around her to find the path back to the lodge.

She made no attempt to stop him.

Dinner was excellent—scallops baked in wine and vegetables fresh from the garden. Afterwards Keith showed slides of a trip he and Anna had taken to Great Slave Lake—Anna supplying the commentary. Lucy didn't attend. Troy went to bed early, and just before he fell asleep remembered the horror in Lucy's face when she'd seen his scar.

She wasn't indifferent to him. He'd swear she wasn't.

He was going to cling to that thought; he needed all the help he could get.

Three days slipped by. Troy went out every day with Stephen and sometimes Hubert, and in the evenings dipped into Keith's library, learning more about the birds he had seen in the daytime. Then a storm blew up and he spent hours watching the surf batter the rocks. When it rained all the next day he taught Stephen his entire repertoire of card tricks.

Anna seemed to be walking a little more heavily, he noticed; in Troy's private opinion she was due earlier than the first of October, the date she'd named.

Troy liked being on an island. Its physical disconnection from the land translated into a sense if not of timelessness at least of time slowing down. With a wisdom that sometimes cost him dearly, because he was impatient and hungry for her, he kept his distance from Lucy and hoped she was growing used to his presence.

He was—almost—content with this. He had no idea what Lucy was feeling. But Hubert soon let him know that he wasn't pleased. Hubert had found out that Troy hadn't been to the owl's nest, so he took him there himself. He then invited Troy in for a drink.

His house was crammed with books about birds, photographs of birds, stuffed birds in various stages of decrepitude, and a motley collection of birds' nests. He poured Troy a generous glass of Drambuie and said, "Well, now you've seen a great horned owl—the major predator on the island. The black-backed gull ranks well below it. By the way, when are you and Lucy getting back together?"

Troy blinked. "I don't know that we are."

"What are you, a man or a mouse?" Hubert demanded with considerable fervor. "She's your wife, isn't she? You waiting for that artist fellow to carry her off? I saw her over there the other day while you were off with Stephen. He's a nice enough man—even if he can't paint—but he's no match for Lucy."

Troy stood stock-still. Perhaps Lucy wasn't getting used to his presence. Perhaps—now that she'd claimed she was getting a divorce—she was getting used to Quentin's instead. His eminently sensible theory that he should give her time smashed into pieces as if he'd dropped his liqueur glass on the stone hearth; jealousy uncurled within him like a venomous snake.

"I haven't met Quentin," he croaked.

"I've got a photo of him somewhere." Hubert rummaged among a pile of papers on a very beautiful oak desk and passed Troy a snapshot. "This was taken at a picnic Anna and Keith gave earlier in the summer."

Against a backdrop of wild roses and deep blue ocean Lucy was standing beside a man who was wearing a brief pair of swim trunks; she was laughing at something he'd just said. The man had the build of an athlete and the good looks of a Greek god.

For some reason Troy had pictured Quentin as balding and middle-aged. His eyes full of primitive antagonism, he said, "That's Quentin?"

"I always thought he was a bit of a cold stick—too much black in the stuff he paints, and he hasn't brought a woman to the island in years. But if anyone can warm his blood, Lucy can. Fight for her, man. Fight! You think I got the money together to buy this island by lying around waiting for someone to drop it in my lap? No, sir. I got out there and I hustled. Time you did the same."

Hubert blew his nose with the trumpeting sound of an old bull elephant and added smugly, "Mrs Mossop's niece is visiting from the mainland. I'll see she helps out in the kitchen—that'll free Lucy up."

The spurious peace of the last few days was gone. His jealousy so intense that he felt as though someone had scourged his flesh with a knife, Troy drained his drink, said his goodbyes, and tramped back to the inn. He'd behaved as stupidly as it was possible to behave. First he'd pushed Lucy into declaring she wanted a divorce, then he'd left her alone for three days so she could celebrate her newly found freedom with a black-haired artist who looked like Adonis. Well done, Troy, he jeered. What's the encore?

He tossed and turned for the rest of the night. But by morning he'd come up with a plan.

After checking with Stephen, he took himself to the kitchen after breakfast. Lucy, looking hot and flushed, was stacking dishes in the sink. She glowered at him. "What do you want?"

Troy lifted a derisive brow at her tone. "If you point me in the right direction I'll make up a couple of packs of sandwiches—Stephen and I are going to the cliffs at the far end of the island."

Rubbing at her forehead with the back of her wrist, she said unwillingly, "It's very beautiful there."

"Why don't you come with us?" he said, as if he'd just thought of the idea. "Stephen can chaperon."

"We don't need a chaperon!" she snapped. "Anyway, I can't. I——"

"Hubert told me Mrs Mossop's niece would be helping in the kitchen. The sun's shining, and you won't be nearly as bad-tempered if you go for a walk in the woods."

"Dr Donovan's sure-fire prescription for cranky women?" Lucy said testily.

"Oh, I could think of other ways of making you less cranky. Where's the bread kept?"

"You're driving me crazy, you know that?"

"Good," said Troy.

"I'd have to be back by four-thirty."

"Stephen will have worn me out long before that—that kid's got the stamina of a mountain goat. The bread, Lucy."

She had picked up a dishtowel and—quite unconsciously, Troy was sure—was wringing it between her hands. Then she blurted, "Do you sometimes look at Stephen and wonder if—if perhaps Michael would have grown up like him?"

It was the first time she had voluntarily spoken Michael's name to Troy in months. "Yes," Troy said steadily. "Yes, I've wondered that more than once." He stepped closer, gently detaching the towel from her fingers. "You'll tear it to shreds, sweetheart," he added, aching with pity for her.

She was staring down at their linked hands, her eyes brilliant with unshed tears. "I don't know what I think about anything any more," she burst out. She yanked her hands free and brushed at her eyes. "Will ham sand-wiches be all right?"

"Sooner or later we'll have to talk about him—Michael, I mean," Troy said. "I'm damned if you and I, of all people, should act as if he never existed."

"Troy, if we're going to fight all the way to the cliffs and back, I won't go!"

"No, you'll hide in the kitchen where it's safe."

"So chicken sandwiches would be more appropriate?" she said, tossing her head.

His smile was ironic. "You look more like a bantam rooster than a chicken. I'd prefer ham."

"With Dijon mustard and mayonnaise and dill pickles."

"So you haven't forgotten the Donovan version of a ham sandwich." He stepped closer, sliding his palms up and down her bare arms. "Do you also remember the way I most liked to make love with you? You'd be wearing that black lace nightgown we bought in Paris, and you'd straddle me and——"

"Stop it—anyone could walk in," Lucy said in a strangled voice. Her cheeks were scarlet and she was looking anywhere but at Troy.

The photograph of Quentin had been engraved on Troy's memory ever since Hubert had shown it to him, and jealousy had been one of the emotions that had kept him awake most of the night. With scant ceremony Troy pulled Lucy toward him and kissed her full on the mouth—a forceful and thorough kiss, to which he brought all the eroticism that the woman in his arms had once shared with him. For a moment Lucy stood like a stick; then she tried to wriggle free of his hold, kicking out at his ankles.

But Troy had had enough of patience and restraint. He tightened the arm around her shoulders, circled her waist with his other arm and deepened his kiss.

With the speed of a lightning bolt snaking through the sky Lucy stopped fighting. Her surrender was so sudden, so complete, and so pliant that Troy was taken unawares. Then, like a second bolt, her own hunger forked to meet his. Troy's heart thudded against his ribs. He clasped her by the hips, distantly aware that her nails were digging into his scalp, into the tendons of his neck and his shoulder muscles; her tongue was dancing against his lips like tiny arrows of fire.

With an inarticulate groan he sought her breast under her apron, its ripe fullness ridding him of the last remnant of control. Then she thrust her body against his groin. Aching to enter her, he muttered her name deep in his throat and thrust back.

"Well, I never!" gasped Mrs Mossop.

With a moan of horror Lucy pushed against Troy's chest. "What am I *doing*? I must be out of my mind!"

"You were as close as you've ever been to making love in the kitchen sink—that's what you were doing," Troy said. Filled with a wild and reckless joy, he began to laugh, and the more furious Lucy looked, and the more scandalized Mrs Mossop, the harder he laughed.

From the doorway Stephen demanded, "What's so funny?"

"I sincerely hope these two are married," Mrs Mossop snorted. "Because if they aren't, they should be. Such goings-on in my kitchen—and in broad daylight, if you please."

Daylight, in Troy's opinion, was the best time. "I do apologize," he said, with minimal sincerity. "Lucy, I'll leave Stephen and Mrs Mossop to help you with the sandwiches—I'll go and get ready. Don't forget the pickles, will you?''

Fifteen minutes later, wearing his oldest, most faded jeans and a blue T-shirt, Troy met up with Stephen on the porch of Lucy's cabin. A couple of minutes later Lucy emerged. She too was wearing jeans—the same tight-fitting ones Troy remembered from their night in the woods with the petrels. Her green cotton shirt, while loose and sporty, couldn't hide the fullness of her breasts or the small hollow at the base of her throat where he had used to rest his cheek after they'd made love and listen to the racing of her pulse slow to normal.

Her eyes were full of animosity, as if she'd read his thoughts. ''Whenever you've finished staring at me we can go.''

He grinned at her. ''How's Mrs Mossop?''

''She didn't actually use the word 'trollop', but I'm sure she was thinking it.''

''I trust you told her I was the instigator?''

Bouncing up and down, Stephen said, ''Let's go!''

''Lead on,'' Lucy said to him, passing Troy the haversack with the lunch.

For her ears alone, Troy added, ''Although by the time she arrived, I think the fact that I was the instigator had become irrelevant.''

Lucy blushed fierily and scurried down the path after Stephen. Troy brought up the rear, and with faint incredulity realized that he was happy. It had been so long that he'd forgotten what it felt like. Nothing was settled; nothing was sure. Nevertheless, he was deeply, wonderfully happy to be here with Lucy—and more than happy to remember that fierce, all-consuming kiss by the kitchen sink. The haversack seemed to weigh nothing, his limbs were alive with energy and he wanted to throw his head back and sing at the top of his lungs.

In deference to the bird population, and to his own tendency to sing off-key, he kept silent. But his heart was singing and, fond though he was of Stephen, he could have wished the boy on the other side of the planet for the rest of the day.

So that he, Troy, could make love with Lucy on that patch of soft green moss lit by the sun among the gently swaying spruce boughs.

They crossed the island, arriving at the west side and beginning the long hike along the rocky beach ridge to the cliffs. Lucy was soon distracted by a big patch of raspberry canes, where the berries hung ripe and heavy and sweet. Stephen was cramming them into his mouth, and Troy's happiness overflowed when Lucy offered him a particularly large one in her fingertips. He bent his head, taking it in his mouth, his eyes fastened on her face.

When she spoke Troy had the sense that she hadn't planned her words at all. As shyly as if she had just met him, rather than having lived with him for four years, she said, "You look—different somehow. Younger."

"I'm happy," he said simply.

"Troy, don't——"

He touched her ruby-stained lips with one finger. "Hush...this isn't the time to worry about tomorrow. I'm happy right now, being here with you. That's more than enough."

"I have everything figured out; I know exactly what I should do—until I'm actually with you," she said jaggedly. "And then it all flies out the window."

"Darling   Lucy,"   Troy   said,   "feed   me another raspberry."

"Darling Troy," she rejoined pertly, "it's your turn to feed me one."

Laughing, he sought among the thorns and the ragged green leaves for a plump, ripe berry, then brushed it along the soft curve of her lower lip until she took it between her teeth. A trickle of juice dripped on to her chin. He wiped if off, wishing his jeans weren't quite so snug, judiciously keeping his back to Stephen. "I'm noticeably ready to substitute the raspberry patch for the kitchen sink," he said.

She glanced down, but although her cheeks warmed to the color of the berries she said primly, "A raspberry patch? Are you into sadomasochism? Your morals are deteriorating, Troy Donovan."

"Such is your power," Troy answered drily.

Stephen said, "You guys look like my mum and dad on their last anniversary—all mushy."

He sounded less than approving. Although Troy had some difficulty imagining Keith being mushy, he meekly stepped back from Lucy and stooped to pick some more berries. Lucy said brightly, "Isn't that a kingbird, Stephen?" and a few minutes later they set out again.

They soon came to the line of rocks called Fishhead Island that lay offshore, with the open ocean beyond it. A narrow tower equipped with a light warned ships of its location. Stephen said, pointing behind him, "See the two rowboats under the trees?"

When Troy looked around he saw two flat-bottomed aluminum boats, lying keel up beneath the spruce trees; oars were stashed under the boats. "What are they for?" he asked.

"It's so the birders can go out to Fishhead. There was a snowy owl there last year, and purple sandpipers, too.

And there's always lots of seals—you can even hear them."

A chorus of sad, protracted moans and groans, interspersed with pugnacious, deep-throated roars was wafting across the strip of ocean. "Anna told me that the story of the sirens is supposed to have originated from the crying of seals," Lucy said. "The sirens who lured men to their doom." She shivered, her face pinched.

With a stab of unease Troy said sharply, "They remind me more of Hubert blowing his nose than of seduction."

"How unromantic of you," Lucy said, and resolutely set off along the beach again.

Did she think she was luring him to his doom? She'd said she wouldn't be responsible were he to get hurt. Troy strode along behind her, his sneakers brushing the tiny pink blooms of herb Robert and the purple spikes of skull-cap. The sow thistle were like gold coins scattered among the rocks, while the ochre-colored seaweed swayed back and forth as the waves rose and fell. Like hair, Troy thought edgily. The hair of a dead woman.

He didn't want to think about doom and death. He was very much alive, as was Lucy; the kiss by the kitchen sink had proved that.

When they came to a long stretch of sand heaped with dried eel grass, Troy had the chance to show off his newly learned expertise in the matter of sandpipers. Then, literally out of the blue, a peregrine falcon streaked the length of the beach, and the pipers erupted as one into the air, wheeling and turning in flashes of dazzling white, like foam flung from the sea. With a sigh of repletion, Stephen said, "Wow."

Further along the shore they took a break, munching on apples from Troy's haversack and playing with the

Frisbee Stephen had been carrying in his own pack.
Stephen's throws were wildly inaccurate; the round plastic
disc spun from his hand with a life of its own, veering
over the beach in tangents that kept Troy and Lucy on
the run.

Troy whipped the Frisbee back to the boy, watching
him jump to grab it out of the air, his shout of triumph
like the cry of a gull. Curving his wrist, Stephen threw
it back with all his strength. Lucy ran to catch it. But
it swerved in mid-air; her eyes glued to it, she chased
after it, her arms outstretched, her long hair blown by
the wind.

The Frisbee—and Lucy—were headed straight for
Troy. He braced himself, and just as his fingers gripped
the curve of plastic, Lucy thudded into his chest. He
staggered a little, his feet losing their purchase on the
sand; instinctively his arms went around her. Laughing
up at him, she said, "It was my turn to catch it!"

She fit perfectly into his body, her tangled hair tickling
his chin, her waist and hip a lissome curve beneath his
arm. Her breasts were crushed against his ribcage. Rather
than loosening his embrace, Troy tightened it in primitive
possessiveness, and watched her eyes darken in a way
he remembered all too well. How many times in their
big bedroom had he watched that same turbulence gather
him in, even as, later, her body would gather him in,
and offer him the intimacy and release that he craved?

The woman in his arms was the woman he'd married;
it was as though the last year and a half was a nightmare
from which he had awakened.

He said, "We mustn't forget we have a chaperon,"
and saw Lucy wrench herself back to the reality of their
surroundings, and the all too obvious betrayal of her
sexual needs. Before she had the chance to pull away

from him he released her, passing her the Frisbee. "You throw it back," he said.

Her hands were trembling as she took it from him, and for a moment she stared at the round piece of plastic as though she wasn't sure what it was. In fierce triumph, Troy thought, You're mine. That hasn't changed—and now you know it as well as I do.

With an erratic sweep of her arm she sent the Frisbee back to Stephen. He raced after it, lunged for it and missed, and with a yell of chagrin tumbled on to the sand on top of it.

As erratically as Lucy's throw, Troy's thoughts carried him onwards, words forming in his brain of their own volition. We're like a family, the three of us—playing together on the sand on a late summer's day... This is what it would have been like if Michael hadn't died.

Deep inside himself he slammed on the brakes. Months ago he had learned there were some trains of thought he couldn't bear to follow because they were too painful; this was one of them.

The Frisbee was winging its way toward him. He caught it automatically and threw it to Lucy, and wasn't sorry when the game broke up a few minutes later. But as they trudged along the shore the sun was still sparkling on the sea, and the wildflowers were dancing among the tall grasses, and Troy's spirits recovered. If he'd told Lucy that for one day she shouldn't worry about tomorrow, then he might also tell himself that for once he should banish yesterday.

Today was more than enough. Because Lucy still wanted him in the most basic way a woman could want a man. How could he be unhappy with that incredible discovery ricocheting through his body?

Shortly afterwards they came to the western edge of the savannah, an expanse of bogs and bright green grass that stretched from one side of the island to the other. "There's a pond on the other shore," Stephen said. "Ducks feed there. But you mustn't try and cross the savannah, Troy. My dad said he'd have my hide if I ever did that. There's sinkholes where you could be sucked under and never be heard of again," he finished with relish.

The savannah looked too beautiful to be dangerous. "I'll keep that in mind," Troy promised.

The cliffs, when they finally arrived, were worth the long walk. Granite escarpments plunged to the sea far below, where they were laced with foam as white as the breast of a gull. The air was loud with the cries of the seabirds perched on the ledges.

Stephen took Troy in hand, pointing out herring gulls, murres and dovekies, and it was Stephen who found the wings and bones of three immature gulls in the grass. The boy said with real excitement, "There must be an owl nesting near here. That's neat. After lunch I'll go and look for it."

"Make sure you stay away from the cliffs," Troy ordered, realizing with another of those twists in his gut that he sounded just like a father.

"They nest in the woods," Stephen said, "not on the cliffs."

Lucy had watched the birds for a while, then unpacked the lunch. They ate seated on the grass back from the cliffs, under the partial shade of some wind-battered spruce trees. "Food always tastes better outdoors," Stephen said contentedly.

Troy smiled at Lucy. "Great ham sandwiches."

She wrinkled her nose. "I've never figured out how anyone can eat dill pickles—let alone lathered with Dijon mustard."

"I'm a man of depraved tastes," he said solemnly. "Or had you forgotten that? Pass the carrot sticks, please, Stephen."

Lucy declined to reply, instead producing a bunch of green grapes and some delicious cherry squares from the pack. Troy ate too much, and afterwards lay back in the grass, his head resting on the haversack. The sun was warm and he felt full and lazy; besides, he'd scarcely slept at all last night. Quentin didn't seem nearly as threatening today as he had yesterday, though. "Wake me in half an hour," he said drowsily.

Stephen was flicking through his bird book while Lucy had wandered away to sit by the edge of the cliffs, and again Troy was aware of how happy he was. The woman sitting with her back to him, watching the gulls soar through the blue sky, was his heart's desire—his one and only love. Everything's going to be all right, he thought. I know it is. And he drifted off to sleep.

CHAPTER FIVE

"TROY—wake *up*! Troy, for heaven's sake, will you please wake up?"

Troy had been dreaming about a covey of beauteous women, all of whom looked like Lucy, who were enticing him down to the rocks, where fat black and white seals lolled in the sun and dove through the waves. He sat up with a jerk, rubbing at his eyes.

Lucy was tugging his arm, her face frantic, her voice a raw plea. "It's Stephen, he's fallen on to one of the ledges——"

His dream vanished as if it had never been. Wide awake, Troy snapped, "On the cliff, you mean? Show me where."

Still holding him by the arm, Lucy half ran across the grass, then dodged between some trees. Her breath was sobbing in her throat and this, more than anything, filled Troy with a cold fear that he couldn't have subdued if his life has depended on it.

He scrambled after her, ducking low beneath the spruce limbs, then skirting a patch of brambles. She stopped dead at the edge of a small patch of grass. "Down there," she whispered, and he saw that she was too frightened to look over the edge.

He strode to the cliff's edge, dropped to his knees and looked over. Stephen was perched precariously on a ledge seven or eight feet down; he had pressed himself against the rough granite face of the cliff. His cheek was scraped and he had been crying. With a thrill of sheer horror

Troy saw that the boy's binoculars had fallen another thirty feet further down the cliff; they were lying smashed beside a gull's nest.

He instantly abandoned any idea he might have had of getting help from the inn, because if the wind came up there was a chance Stephen could lose his grip and fall. Doing his best to ignore how very far away the frill of white foam looked, he said matter-of-factly, "Stephen, I'm going to lie flat and get Lucy to hold my ankles. Then I'll lift you up, okay? You'll have to hold on as hard as you can."

Stephen shifted his cheek enough to meet Troy's eyes. "Okay," he said in a thin voice.

Troy lay flat on his belly, twisting his head to look back at Lucy. "Grab my ankles and hold on—then pull back when I tell you to. It'll be all right, sweetheart, we'll have him up here in no time—the ledge isn't that far down."

Her face set, Lucy nodded, and fastened her hands on Troy's ankles so hard that they felt like leg irons. Troy crawled forward until his head and shoulders were over the cliff, carefully judging how far he could go without losing his balance; reaching down with both hands, he seized the boy by the wrists. Grinning at him, he said, "Good thing I did weight-lifting all summer— up we go, Stephen."

Stephen was heavier than he looked, and gravity was against them. Feeling the strain in his shoulders, Troy hauled upward with all his strength, his biceps as hard as the rock that was digging into his belly. "Pull, Lucy," he panted, and began inching back from the edge of the cliff. Stephen dug his toes into the granite, trying to help by levering himself as best he could.

Sweat springing out on his forehead, his wrists aching, Troy dragged himself still further back, feeling the rough granite scour the undersides of his arms. The sharp-pointed fragment of a shell was digging into his ribs; if he'd had any sense he would have brushed the rocks off first. Grimacing from the pain, he decided Lucy must be sitting on his ankles with her whole weight. Shin splint, anyone? he thought crazily, and with a gargantuan tug gained another six precious inches.

Once more, Troy... you can do it.

Filling his lungs, he grunted, "Give it all you've got, Lucy," and with a combination of a tug and a twist that he wouldn't have wanted to repeat, because it ripped at every muscle in his torso, he saw Stephen flop forward on to the grass.

Troy rolled over on to his back, his breath heaving in his chest, and pulled the boy into his arms. Now that Stephen was safe, the vertigo of that sheer drop to the waves below brought a surge of nausea into his throat.

Stephen burst into tears; Lucy, crouched at Troy's feet, did likewise. Somehow Troy managed to sit up, still holding the boy tightly to his side, and reached out for Lucy. But she struck his hand away and cried all the harder. "He's safe," Troy gasped. "I couldn't have done that without your help, Lucy."

"He could have been killed," Lucy sobbed. "D-dead like Michael."

"Well, he's not," Troy said grimly, fighting down another wave of sickness. "Although I'd like to know what the devil you were doing near the cliff, Stephen, when you told us you were going to look for the owl's nest."

Stephen pulled free of Troy, scrubbed at his face with a dirty hand, and gingerly extracted a feather from the pocket of his jeans. It was a very pretty feather, softly marbled in gray and rust. "I saw this just over the edge of the cliff," he said. "But when I reached for it, it blew further down and I slipped." His breath caught in a hiccup in his throat. "It's an owl's feather," he finished, with a wavering grin of triumph. "I don't have any owl feathers in my collection."

"You very nearly didn't have that one," Troy announced. "You did a really stupid and dangerous thing, Stephen—you know that, don't you?"

All the pleasure fled from Stephen's face. He nodded, shamefaced. "Are you going to tell my dad?"

"I'll have——"

"Of course we'll have to tell your parents," Lucy snapped.

Stephen edged closer to Troy, who put his arm around him again. "I didn't mean to scare you, Lucy," the boy gulped.

She said, glaring at the two of them impartially, "I was awake the whole time, sitting by the cliff. You must have sneaked behind me, Stephen, to end up where you did."

"I didn't sneak," Stephen protested, his lip quivering. "I found the nest in the woods, and the place where I came out was where I saw the feather."

"You're not to be trusted," she flared.

"Can it, Lucy," Troy said flatly.

"Don't you tell me what to do!"

"Lay off," he said in a hard voice. "Stephen got a bad scare, and I'll be willing to bet that when he sees the next owl feather he'll think twice before he tries to add it to his collection... And now we'd better head out; he's got a couple of nasty scraps that I'll have to take a look at when we get back to the inn."

At some point in his escapade Stephen had lost a fair portion of skin from one knee, and there were tiny flecks of dirt ground into the wound; the graze on his cheek, while less serious, was far from clean. The boy was still clinging to Troy in a way that filled him with bittersweet emotions—emotions he wasn't sure he wanted Lucy, in her present mood, to see.

Trying to calm down, Troy went on, "If you could carry the haversack, Lucy, I'll take Stephen on my back."

Without a word Lucy slung the pack over her shoulder and set off through the trees. Troy knelt, so Stephen could climb on his back, then started after her. And as he hiked along the shoreline, Stephen's thin hands clamped around his neck, he decided that before the day was done he and Lucy were going to have a talk. He'd had enough of evasions and silence in the last year and a half. More than enough. Tonight Lucy could spell out for him exactly why she'd lost her temper back there at the cliff.

He had a pretty good idea what it had been about.

Nevertheless, he thought, it should make for an interesting conversation. Certainly not a polite one, if he had anything to do with it.

It was nine o'clock that evening before Troy saw the soft glow of light coming through the windows of Lucy's cabin. Noticing that she'd drawn every one of the curtains tight shut, he pulled on a sweater over his shirt and went downstairs.

When they'd gotten back to the inn that afternoon Stephen had been roundly reprimanded by Anna, and even Keith had added a few well-chosen words. Troy had cleaned the boy's scrapes and bandaged them. Lucy had disappeared into the kitchen and Mrs Mossop had served dinner, treating Troy with a frigid politeness that at another time he might have found funny.

Now he padded soft-footed across the springy ground to Lucy's cabin and knocked on the door. He was more than half prepared to find that she'd bolted it against him. However, she flung the door wide open and said, "I was expecting you—come in."

So for the second time Troy stepped into the little cabin where Lucy lived. The other thing he'd half expected was that she would choose the beach or the woods for the confrontation that she, as much as he, had known was coming ever since they'd left the cliffs. Not the cabin, where the double bed seemed to be right in front of him no matter which way he looked.

Was she so sure of herself, so inured against him, that she didn't even care that he was in her bedroom?

This wasn't a thought calculated to calm Troy's temper. He said evenly, "May I sit down?"

"This won't take long," Lucy said.

Oh, won't it? thought Troy. He pulled out a wooden chair and straddled it, resting his arms on the back. "Why don't you start?" he said. "You look like you're only too ready."

She leaned against the back of the room's sole armchair and for a moment regarded him in silence. In spite of himself, his nerves tightened. You're fighting for your life, he reminded himself. Keep your cool.

"I want you to leave," Lucy said. "There's a boat coming out from the mainland tomorrow with supplies; you could go back on it. I don't want you here, Troy."

With a huge effort Troy kept his hands relaxed on the smooth wood; his instant, crushing disappointment told him more clearly than words that in his heart of hearts—

and against all the odds—he had hoped for something else. "Explain yourself," he said.

"I shouldn't have to—I've said it all before."

"What happened at the cliffs, Lucy?"

"You don't miss a trick, do you?"

"Not where you're concerned, no."

She said, choosing her words with cold precision, "If you don't miss a trick, then you know that I was enjoying the day up until then. That I liked being with you and Stephen——"

All Troy's good intentions evaporated. "Don't bracket me with Stephen! Surely to God I mean more to you than him."

"Shut up and listen," Lucy fumed. "It was fun picking raspberries and playing Frisbee and picnicking on the rocks. But then——"

"Was it fun kissing me in the raspberry patch, Lucy? Was that fun, too?"

"Yes," she said, with a rebellious lift of her chin, "it was. You can be—very persuasive. But there's a lot more at stake here than just a day spent in the outdoors having fun. Stephen could have been killed on the cliffs, Troy— we both know that. That's why I want you to leave. Because I'll never risk that kind of pain again."

He said, stating the obvious, "What happened on the cliffs brought Michael's death back to you."

She dropped her gaze. "Of course it did."

"But it had a happy ending."

"It could very easily not have—be realistic!"

She was right; he knew it as well as she. Troy leaned forward, his whole body focusing on what he was about to say, because each word would weave the fabric of the kind of truth that didn't often get spoken—a truth he hadn't even known was his until now.

"I want a family, Lucy. Another child. I know that in my bones. Yeah, I fantasized today, when the three of us were out there on the beach... We were like a family spending their holidays together." He took a deep breath. "But I'll tell you something else. More than a family, I want you. You alone. My wife. Back in my bed, in my home, in my life. For the rest of my life. And if that means no family, so be it."

Lucy moved involuntarily, and as she did so the lamplight shot through the shining mass of her hair. "Oh, Troy..." she whispered, and for a moment he thought he had won.

But then, clasping her hands in front of her, her face very pale, she went on with desperate sincerity, "I couldn't do that to you—it would be the cruelest deprivation in the world, and you deserve so much more. Don't think me blind, please, Troy. I remember what a good father you were to Michael, and I've watched you with Stephen ever since you got here—you're made to be a father. But I'm too afraid to have another child. You've got to believe me and move on."

"There are ways we can ensure we'd never have any more children," he said levelly. "And then you'd be safe."

Her knuckles white, Lucy said, "You'd end up hating me."

He stood up, the chair-legs rasping on the floor. "No, I wouldn't—I couldn't. I love you too much for that."

With a tiny gesture she warded him off. "I can't stand this, Troy! I won't do that to you—cut you off from fatherhood. *Please*...get on the boat tomorrow and leave me alone."

For a moment Troy wavered. Was she right? Was he beating his head against a brick wall by staying here?

After all, it took two people to effect a reconciliation, and not once in the last twelve months had Lucy said she loved him. If he were sensible he'd leave the cabin right now and the island tomorrow.

You're a quitter, Troy, a little voice sneered in his ear. I thought you were fighting for your life.

He walked around the chair and let the back of it take his weight, his long legs splayed in front of him. Then he said casually, "I don't think I mentioned that I've been offered a new job. In Arizona. One that in terms of upward mobility I'd be a fool to turn down—I have to let them know in the next couple of days what I'm going to do. One reason I came here was because I felt you should be part of that decision."

He had taken her by surprise. "I've just made it clear to you that I'm not," she said shortly.

"I'd have to sell the house, of course," he went on, as if she hadn't spoken. "It's in both our names, so you'd have to sign your consent and then you'd get half the proceeds."

In a choked voice she said, "I don't want your money, Troy. I've told you that before."

"This money you'll have to take. You can give it to a home for stray cats or you can throw it in the Rideau Canal—I don't give a damn what you do with it! But you'll legally be required to take it."

She said stringently, "I remember not long after we met you told me I was argumentative and contentious. That's nothing compared to the way you behave, Troy Donovan. I would have thought 'no' was a fairly simple word to understand. Just two letters, only one syllable—nothing difficult about that. But for some reason you're deaf to it." Her voice was rising, for Lucy had never been the most even-tempered of women. "Will you kindly get out of here this minute?"

"You were the one to invite me in." He let his eyes wander over to the bed. "To talk, of course. That's all."

"Leave right now," she gritted, "or I'll go and get Keith."

"I can't imagine Keith being able to persuade me to leave verbally," Troy remarked. "If he says 'good morning' he's used up half his stock of words for the day. And, as I'm both taller and stronger than he is, a more direct means of removal is out of the question. Although I suppose you might try enlisting Hubert's help...that could be fun."

"Out!" she yelped.

"When I sell the house, which pieces of furniture will you want, Lucy? And what about the painting I gave you in Provence? Your collection of seashells? The cushions you embroidered?" With deliberate brutality he added, "I guess I'd have to sell the nursery furniture, wouldn't I?"

In a low voice she said, "I hate you." She pushed away from the chair and walked past him toward the door. "If you won't leave, then I will."

Troy stood up, making no attempt to stop her. He said, "Do you know what's so awful here, Lucy? You remember what I was like when we met in Tortola? My sister had died a few months before that and I was so caught up in rage that I couldn't mourn her as she deserved. But you cured me. You freed me to weep for her, so that I was able to let her go. You did that for me."

He raked his fingers through his hair and finished with a depth of bitterness that made her flinch. "I have a hell of a time accepting the fact that I haven't been able to do the same thing for you. That I can't help you in any

way that counts. Other than getting out of your life and
never coming back.''

Standing stock-still by the door, Lucy said unsteadily,
"I never met your sister, Troy, so I was to some extent
detached—perhaps that's why I could help. But Michael
was ours—our own son." She stared down at the floor.
"You mustn't blame yourself that I ran away...it wasn't
your fault.''

Her sudden capitulation drained him more than her
anger. Troy said, walking closer, "I was the one who
precipitated your leaving—by suggesting we had another
child. Remember? I thought the best thing for both of
us would be another baby in the nursery—something to
fill that dreadful emptiness." He raked his fingers
through his hair again. "Not one of my smartest moves.
It was much too soon—I see that now. But that was
when we had the fight—the worst fight of our whole
marriage. The next day you were gone.''

"You asked for the one thing I couldn't give you! I
still can't.''

Not nearly as sure of the truth of his words as he
sounded, Troy said, "But you still love me.''

"That's got nothing to do with it.''

"It's got everything to do with it!'' he exploded in
total frustration.

Her hand was on the door-latch. Once he would have
taken her in his arms with all the confidence of a man
who knew himself both loved and desired. Now—
despising himself—Troy watched his fingers reach out
tentatively to touch a strand of her hair, his simple need
for recognition conquering his fear of rejection.

Her stillness took on another quality—that of the
trapped animal who saw the hunter approach and knew
itself helpless. She was suffering his touch, he thought

savagely. Out of compassion—perhaps even out of the remnants of love. "Don't pity me, Lucy," he said.

"I pity us both," she answered, so quietly that he had to strain to hear her.

His anger vanished and his words came out without forethought. "When you left, I went on a three-day drunk. I surfaced feeling as though I'd spent ten rounds in the ring with Muhammad Ali." His smile was twisted. "I'm beginning to feel the same way again. You don't have to leave—I'll go." With exquisite poignancy he traced the line of her cheek to the corner of her mouth. "I expected far too much of you. Your child had died, and six months later I asked you to have another one. I never meant to hurt you more than you'd been hurt, Lucy—I'm truly sorry."

For the first time since she'd flung the door open to let him in, Lucy's eyes filled with tears. "Goodnight, Troy," she faltered.

Troy opened the door and stepped out into the warm, fragrant darkness. The moon had risen over the water while he'd been inside—a waxing moon, full of promise for the perfection to come. As exhausted as if he'd spent two hours lifting weights, Troy stood irresolutely, hearing the door close behind him. Tired, he might be. Ready to go to bed, he wasn't.

He walked down to the beach and perched on a rock overlooking the water, where the moonlight shimmered, white on black. Life wasn't like that, he thought. Life was all the shades of gray. Murky and incomprehensible.

For a man who knew exactly what he wanted, he wasn't getting any closer to his goal.

At breakfast the next morning Mrs Mossop announced that the supply boat would be at the dock in an hour if anyone had mail to go to the mainland. Troy chewed his way through eggs Benedict that tasted like sawdust and then went to Anna and Keith's apartment to change the dressing on Stephen's knee. The wound looked clean, and Stephen none the worse for wear. His shelves housed an orderly assortment of shells, feathers and rocks; there was a stack of books by his bed.

"Dad grounded me," he said. "I'm not allowed out for two whole days. If you see the owl, you'll tell me, won't you, Troy?"

To keep Stephen cooped within the four walls of his room for two days was punishment indeed. "Sure," said Troy. He'd never really intended getting on the supply boat this morning—had he?

As Anna put away the first-aid kit she said warmly, "Thanks, Troy."

She was pushing a strand of hair back from her face. He heard himself say, "You don't blame me and Lucy for Stephen's escapade?"

"Oh, no," she said in evident surprise. "Ever since he learned to walk he's been getting into trouble—he has all the instincts of an explorer without any of the common sense. I'm just so grateful to both of you for getting him off the cliff."

Her belly looked swollen out of all proportion to her small-boned frame. "How are you feeling?" Troy asked.

"Tired," she answered with a faint smile. "This last two weeks feels like forever."

"I'm no obstetrician, but it looks to me like you could go sooner."

"I don't think so," she said confidently. "I was late with Stephen."

"When are you going to the mainland?"

"Next week. I have a sister I can stay with until the baby's born." She tidied Stephen's pile of books, kissed her son on the cheek, and led the way out into the hall. "Lucy mentioned you'd be leaving this morning. I'll get Keith to make up your bill."

Lucy was very sure of herself, Troy thought with a hot stab of anger. Then an idea flashed through his brain. An idea that was both unscrupulous and dishonest. An idea he was going to act on. He said, "I'm not leaving, no. But would you do me a favor, Anna? If Lucy asks, would you tell her that, as far as you know, I've gone?"

Anna looked at him from cool dark eyes. "If Lucy really doesn't want to be married to you, you've got no right to harass her."

It was not a viewpoint Hubert would have espoused. With painful accuracy Troy said, "I think she still loves me. Maybe this way I'll find out."

Anna said reluctantly, "You'd better move your things from your room, then—she's the one who'd be cleaning it."

Feeling like a louse, because he was sure Anna was helping him only because he'd rescued Stephen the day before, Troy said, "Thanks."

After he'd gone back to his room, he wrote out a brief message for the institute in Arizona and put it in an envelope along with some money. He piled all his gear into his bag and stuffed it in the closet of the empty room next door. Then he walked down to the dock.

Clarence was off-loading boxes of groceries from the dinghy, while Keith was piling the supplies on a little motorized trailer parked at the top of the slip. Glad of the exercise, Troy tramped back and forth with cartons of fruit and vegetables. When all the food was loaded,

Keith nodded his thanks, said goodbye and drove off toward the inn.

Troy passed Clarence the envelope and explained what he wanted. "No sweat," Clarence said cheerfully. "Your gear here? Keith figured you were headin' out."

"No," Troy said. "I'm staying at least another week."

"You kin give me a shove off the wharf, then—wait, now, here comes Hubert."

Hubert was scurrying toward the slip, waving a bundle of letters. "Battery quit in my alarm clock," he puffed. "Didn't realize it until I saw the time at Anna's. Nearly missed you, Clarence. How are you? You still here, Troy? Not loading your wife on the boat to take her home? You disappoint me." He gave an uncouth laugh and began explaining the postage on his letters to Clarence. Afterward, he and Troy pushed the dinghy down the slip and Clarence took off in a swirl of foam.

"So," said Hubert. "The rumor round the inn this morning was that you were leaving."

"I'm not," Troy said economically.

"She's being a mite stubborn?"

"She'd say I was the one being stubborn."

"Humph," said Hubert. "I never did get married. But if I had, I'd have wanted a woman with spirit. Trouble is, a woman with spirit isn't always going to do what you want her to do. Let me think about this." Frowning prodigiously, he stared out at *Four Angels*, where she was swaying on the swell.

Troy watched the waves slurp at his boots; the tide was rising. Hubert said, "You could've gone to the kitchen, thrown her over your shoulder, dumped her in the dinghy and taken off. That would've solved everything."

"It would have put me in jail," Troy retorted. "The days when the baron could ride off into the sunset with the beautiful maiden draped across his saddle are long gone, Hubert."

"We knew where we were then," Hubert snorted. "Men were men, and there was none of this equality stuff."

"Any number of women would take strong exception to that statement. Especially women with spirit."

Hubert produced an enormous white handkerchief from his pocket and blew his nose stentoriously. "I think you should go see Quentin," he pronounced. "I know I'm just an old man who's been a bachelor all his life— but if I had to lay a bet, I'd say there's not enough heat between Lucy and Quentin to melt an ice-cream on a hot day. But you should check it out. Just in case. You can't trust those artist fellows. Models and red wine and all that north light."

He paused in reflection. "I'd say Lucy's got too much sense. But there's no accounting for taste, is there? And women do some funny things. You know how to find his place?"

Quentin wasn't Troy's top priority. But Hubert in his own way was doing his best to be helpful, so Troy took the little map drawn on the back of an envelope that Hubert passed him a few moments later and put it in his pocket. "Let me know what you find out," Hubert said, bright-eyed as a heron sighting a frog. "And watch yourself today; the fog's going to roll in before too long."

Troy had noticed the thick band of gray cowering at the horizon. "There was a moon last night," he remarked.

"The weather changes here between one minute and the next. And the fog can be thicker than the down

feathers on an eider duck. Not something to fool with.''
With a decisive nod Hubert tugged the flaps straight on
his jacket and marched off toward the lighthouse.

Troy stayed where he was, listening to the water gurgle
through the wooden slats. He didn't want to go and see
Quentin—an artist who looked like a Greek god and who
had laughed with Lucy in the summer sunshine.

Anna's words were circling in his mind and wouldn't
go away; Anna thought Lucy had the right to be left
alone. Maybe Anna knew something he didn't. Maybe
he was way off base even to imagine that Lucy still loved
him. After all, she'd put the width of the country between
herself and Troy this summer; that was scarcely the behavior of a loving wife.

Maybe—despite his own brave words—Lucy was
falling in love with Quentin.

Feeling depressed and out of sorts, Troy hiked along
the shore in the opposite direction to the lighthouse for
the better part of an hour. On the way back he found
himself keeping to the shelter of the trees, although the
more he thought about his stratagem to deceive Lucy
the more shabby and ineffectual it seemed. A grown man
trying to creep up on his wife, to take her by surprise?
It was time he went home to Vancouver. At least in the
hospital he knew what his role was, and he could ac-
complish something useful. All he was doing here was
acting like a lovesick adolescent.

A bird flitted across the trail ahead of him; luckily
Stephen didn't know he was out here without his binoculars. The bird—whatever it was—was stirring up the
dead leaves on the forest floor, making as much noise
as if it were a racoon. As Troy peered through the trees
something small and brown flew deeper into the forest.
A great many birds were small and brown. Knowing all

too well that he was trying to distract himself from thoughts of Lucy, Troy walked soft-footed round a corner in the path and stopped with a jerk, as if he'd been shot.

Lucy was standing not twenty feet from him. The trail had opened out into a view of the ocean; she was leaning against a gnarled old spruce tree as though she needed its support, her shoulders drooping, her cheek resting against the rough bark. She looked exhausted. No, worse than exhausted, Troy thought slowly. Defeated. Diminished. And he realized even then that he hadn't found quite the right word for the slump of her body and her utter immobility.

He knew something else. He had intruded on a moment of intense privacy. Lucy had walked this far from the lodge because she wanted to be alone with her feelings. The best, if not the only thing he could do for her was to leave her to her solitude.

He looked over his shoulder to check his footing, spruce boughs brushing his arm. With a loud squawk a jay perched in the maple tree across the path flung itself into the air, and like a blue arrow streaked toward the beach. Lucy's head turned.

She couldn't have failed to see him. His mind a blank, his long legs covering the ground all too fast, Troy walked up to her.

The color had drained from her face. She looked as though she was about to faint. Worse, he thought numbly, she looked the same as she had the day Michael died. Her eyes were sunk in their sockets, with bruised shadows beneath them. Her jaw was clenched, her soft lips compressed, as though to hold back a scream that if once started would never end.

He muttered, "Lucy... Oh, God, Lucy," and blindly reached out for her.

She was clutching the bark as if it were the only thing that was keeping her upright. In a shocked whisper she said, "You left. Keith told me."

"I—I changed my mind."

It was quite clear she hadn't heard him. "You didn't say goodbye. You left without saying goodbye."

"Lucy, I—"

"I had to clean your room—Anna's so tired, I couldn't let her do it." In a cracked voice, the words dragged from her, she said, "I even had to change your bed."

"Lucy, please——"

Her eyes had filmed with tears; her lower lip was trembling. "The sheets, the pillowcases—I held them to my face and I swear I could catch the s-scent of your b-body."

This was worse than anything Troy could have imagined. "Lucy, don't——"

But she overrode him, and again he was quite sure she hadn't heard a word he'd said. Not, he thought ferociously, that he'd said anything worth saying. He sounded like a cracked record. Lucy, Lucy, Lucy...

"Why did you stay?" she quavered, scrubbing at her eyes with the back of her hand and pushing away from the tree trunk. "You changed your mind—why?"

Troy said hoarsely, knowing that the only way he could possibly make amends was to tell her the exact truth, "I never intended going. I wanted to see if——"

"It was a trick? A game?" she croaked.

"Lucy, it was the stupidest thing I could have——"

"You did it on *purpose*? You manipulated me into thinking you'd gone without even saying goodbye, and all the time you were skulking around here watching me?"

Stung, he protested, "It was pure accident that I came across you. When I did see you, I tried to leave without you knowing I was here."

"You expect me to believe that? I may be stupid, Troy, but I'm not that stupid."

"I went for a walk along the shore because I didn't know what else to do with myself—I wasn't spying on you!"

Where her cheeks had been as pale as moonlight, they were now flushed like an evening sky. "You sure have changed in the last year. You were never dishonest with me—never. How could I ever trust you now?"

"Since you don't want anything to do with me, that's surely an academic question," Troy retorted, with more accuracy than good sense.

She swept on, "I've never in my life advocated violence; I deplore it as a way of settling disputes. But I'll tell you, I wish I were Muhammad Ali right now—if I had you against the ropes I'd make mincemeat out of you. Do you have any idea what you've put me though in the last two hours?"

Through a welter of shame, anger and regret, Troy pounced. "Why don't you tell me about it?" he said.

Lucy's eyes widened; she let out her breath in a long sigh. "That's why you did it," she said in a dazed voice. "To see if I'd care if you left."

"And you did care, didn't you? You cared a whole lot."

"So it worked, your little trick—I guess I should congratulate you on your cleverness, shouldn't I?" Each word like a drop of acid on his skin, she went on, "Do you know how I feel? I feel as though I've been stripped naked in front of a roomful of strangers.''

A muscle twitched in Troy's jaw. "Is that how you see me—as a stranger?''

''I hate what you did to me this morning—making a fool of me like that! You can stay on this island as long as you like—but you and I are through. I don't want to talk to you, I don't want you coming near my cabin, and I don't want you playing any more of your cute little tricks on me. Neither——'' her eyes narrowed ''—do I want you following me right now. I'm going for a walk. Go back to the inn, Troy. Unpack your bags and settle into your room again. Do whatever you like—but stay out of my way!''

Keeping a careful distance between them, she stalked round him and set off at a brisk clip down the shore, in the direction from which he'd come. Her hips swung from side to side in her jeans.

Troy watched her go, and through a confusion of emotions he couldn't possibly have categorized heard the singing of one pure, clean note: Lucy still loves me.

She was angrier with him than she'd ever been in her life. She despised him for the trick he'd pulled. But underneath it all she loved him. Loved and desired him.

The trick had worked.

It was more than he deserved.

CHAPTER SIX

TRUE to Hubert's predictions, the fog rolled in after lunch—a fog so thick it was like drizzle. Troy played cards with Stephen some of the afternoon, then went to his room to read. He didn't want to think about Lucy—mostly because he had no idea what he was going to do next. For a man who could put a string of letters after his name, he had behaved with a singular lack of integrity once already today. For the rest of the day he was going to lie low.

The latest Tom Clancy was just what he needed. When a tap came at his door, late in the afternoon, it took him a moment to come back to reality from the world of espionage and CIA agents. "Come in," he called, certain that whoever wanted to see him it wouldn't be Lucy.

Anna opened the door, leaning on the handle. Troy said quickly, "Are you all right?"

"You're worse than Keith," she said. "I'm fine. I was just wondering if you knew where Lucy was."

"No. I haven't seen her since this morning."

With a worried frown Anna said, "She should have been in the kitchen an hour ago. She's very dependable; it's not like her to be late."

"You mean she's missing?" Anxiety racing along his nerves, Troy swung his legs over the side of the bed and stood up. "You've checked her cabin? What about Hubert or Quentin—could she be there?"

"I called Quentin on the cellular phone; he hasn't seen her at all today. Keith talked to Hubert—same thing.

Stephen's been in his room all day and Mrs Mossop hasn't seen her since breakfast. The birders are downstairs by the fireplace, because the fog's so thick they couldn't see where they were going.''

Troy said flatly, ''The last I saw of Lucy she was headed along the shore toward the cliffs.'' With painful exactitude he confessed, ''She was really upset by the trick I pulled—I should never have pretended I was leaving.''

''I saw her after she'd cleaned your room; she looked terrible.'' Anna paled. ''The cliffs could be dangerous in the mist.''

An ice-cold fist had clenched around his heart. ''I'm sure she'd be careful there because of what happened to Stephen. But she could have lost her bearings in the fog, Anna.''

''She knows how treacherous the swamps are... Surely she'd stay away from the savannah?''

The fist closed tighter round Troy's heart. ''Stephen warned us about the sinkholes only yesterday.''

''Keith exaggerated a bit, to make sure Stephen wouldn't try crossing the savannah on his own. But it's no place to be on a day like this.''

Troy reached for his jacket on the back of the door. ''I'm going out to look for her. If I cover this shore and the eastern half of the savannah, could Keith do the west side?''

''Yes. And I'll call Quentin; he can go along the petrel trails and the area around the lighthouse. I'll ask the birders to help too; they could go to the heron roosts inland.'' Unexpectedly Anna rested a hand on Troy's sleeve. ''Try not to blame yourself, Troy.''

''Is it that obvious?''

"It's very obvious how much you love her," Anna said gently. "Take a flashlight, won't you? Keith has a big siren—he'll sound it when she's found."

Troy put a flashlight and an extra sweater in his haversack, and downstairs added a Thermos of coffee and some chocolate bars. He had a quick chat with Keith, to coordinate their routes, and after lacing up his hiking boots at the back door he stepped outside.

The fog was like a presence in itself, thick and impenetrable, and for a moment he panicked. He'd be lucky if he could find the trail, let alone Lucy.

He had to find her. Because he was, despite what Anna had said, responsible for Lucy's plight.

Troy set off along the path to the beach, and from there picked up the trail that led along the ridge of the shoreline. The mist had shrunk the world to a small circle of clarity that traveled with him. Trees loomed to meet him while the sea, even though it was close enough that he could hear the waves splashing and bubbling around the rocks, was invisible; this gave him a peculiar sense of isolation, of being cut off from all that was familiar. As though, he thought, there was no one else in the world but him. As though Lucy had never existed.

Cursing himself for being overly imaginative, Troy kept to the line of tamped-down earth that wound between the trees, stopping every few feet to shout Lucy's name as loudly as he could. But the fog swallowed his voice, deadening it in its white shroud. Lucy could be no distance away and she wouldn't hear him. He fought down a fear that if he allowed it rein would destroy him, and tramped on.

His jeans were soon soaked to the knee, where the weeds and grasses brushed against them, his jacket was pearled with moisture and his hair was clinging to his forehead. Lucy had only been wearing a short-sleeved T-shirt with her jeans, and she hadn't been carrying anything to eat or drink. Again he yelled her name, and as he stood still waiting felt the silence press against his ears.

He took to the beach ridge, his boots skidding on the wet rocks. A herring gull wailed from the shoreline, and through the fog Troy heard the mournful peal of a bell from one of the channel markers. It sounded as though it was tolling for the dead, he thought with an inner shiver, and shouted Lucy's name in defiance of something he couldn't have named. And then he saw the gnarled spruce tree take shape ahead of him; the last time he had seen it, Lucy had been standing beneath it.

She wasn't there now.

He marched on, all his senses alert. He knew Lucy had gone this way; he'd watched her only a few hours ago. He called her name more often, stopping and listening with every ounce of his concentration for the slightest of sounds, his eyes flicking from side to side along the trail for any mark of her passage. He passed the clump of boulders where he and Stephen had one day seen a flock of eider ducks and four loons; he passed the narrow, winding pathway that led to the heron roosts. The birders would be checking there. His job was to keep to the shoreline.

When he came to the pond that Stephen had told him about, Troy bellowed, "Lucy!" as loudly as he could. A pair of green-winged teal burst into the air, startling him, veering away from him to vanish in the mist. His heart pounding, he realized they had told him something: Lucy wasn't anywhere in the vicinity of the pond.

The trail left the beach for the woods again, then the trees thinned. His throat tightening, Troy realized he had reached the savannah, the swampy meadow that stretched from one side of the island to the other. According to Anna it wasn't as dangerous as Stephen had said, but just an hour ago Keith had warned Troy to be careful should he venture into it.

Troy skirted the edge of the meadow, forcing himself to take his time even though logic was telling him that Lucy had probably gone straight to the cliffs to watch the seabirds and that he should hurry. Then he stopped in his tracks. The plume of a goldenrod had been bent to the ground; footprints indented the flattened grass. Twice he yelled Lucy's name, straining to hear through the fog.

Nothing.

The footprints were headed straight into the savannah. Human footprints. One of the birders, oblivious to the dangers of the swamp? Or Lucy, seeing something new and exciting and impulsively deciding to take a closer look?

It wouldn't be the first time.

Keith had given Troy a roll of bright red plastic tape for use if he left the trail. Unwinding it, Troy anchored the end with a small pile of rocks and began following the footprints, the tape straggling behind him. When he looked around four or five minutes later, he was heartily grateful for Keith's forethought; with no landmarks, no slope to the beach or trail between the trees, he could only too easily have lost his way and blundered around in the clumps of grass—all of which looked alike—until the fog chose to lift.

The silence was so absolute as to be eerie. If Lucy was anywhere in the vicinity her imagination would be working overtime; Troy knew her well enough for that. He himself had to fight the tendency to keep looking back over his shoulder, as though unknown eyes were watching him. Hostile eyes, resentful of intruders.

The grasses had narrowed to a bridge between two large oval puddles of mud and Troy realized he had lost sight of the footprints. Castigating himself for not paying attention, he backtracked, now not sure which were the marks he had left and which were those of the person he was following. Trying to think, feeling fear batter at his composure, because it seemed all too likely that Lucy was lost somewhere ahead of him and it was up to him to find her, he decided to go back to the narrow bridge of grass. It had widened to more solid ground; perhaps there he could pick up the traces again.

He picked his way across the bridge with care, the swamp squelching under his heels. When his footing felt more secure, he stooped to check the grass for prints. There seemed to be two sets, as though someone had wandered in circles.

Letting out more tape, Troy traipsed back and forth across the clearing. On the far side a cluster of spiky white orchids, their fringed petals jeweled with dew, poked upward through the grass. That, he thought, could well have been Lucy's quarry. There was another patch of flowers just ahead of him. He jumped over the intervening peat and shouted for Lucy once again.

From his left came an answering call, like the keening of a marshbird.

His heart began to race in his chest, threatening to deafen him. "Lucy!" he yelled. "Lucy?"

The sound was clearer this time. Trying to pinpoint it in the mist, Troy headed in that direction, balancing on hummocks of reeds, leaping from clump to clump across a stagnant stream that smelled richly of sulfur. He stopped suddenly, realizing with a fierce jolt of hope that somehow he had found the trail again; in front of him were three footprints that definitely weren't his own.

And then he heard the one voice he had been searching for ever since Anna had told him that Lucy hadn't turned up for dinner. Lucy's voice, calling, "Troy, I'm over here—be careful; I'm right by a sinkhole."

He couldn't see her yet; but he could hear her. Picking his way with painstaking caution, he headed toward the elusive sound of her voice.

"Here!" she called again.

Troy could see her now, a crouched figure in the wet grass. For a moment he stood still, pervaded by a mute and passionate gratitude that she was alive. Then he crossed the last barrier of grass and mud and knelt beside her.

She threw herself into his arms, burrowed her face into his chest and clung to him with all her strength. His gratitude blossoming into such a certainty of love that he was shaken to the core, Troy held her close. She was shivering. Trying to wrap his warmth around her, he said, "It's all right, sweetheart, you're safe... It's all right."

Her soaked curls were butting his chin. Her arms were hard around his ribcage, her breasts crushed to his chest. Wondering dazedly if it were possible to die of happiness, Troy let his cheek rest on her wet hair. I love you... I love you... The words repeated themselves in his head over and over again. But how could he say them, when only that morning Lucy had vowed she wanted nothing more to do with him?

As if she had read his mind, Lucy lifted her head. Her eyes a drowned, stormy gray, she cried, "Troy, what are we going to *do*?"

"I'm going to get a sweater out of my haversack, put it on you, and give you a cup of hot coffee," he said, smiling at her with all the love in his heart.

"When you look at me like that, I want to bawl my head off," she wailed. "I don't mean now. I mean about us."

He said with complete truth, "I don't know, Lucy—I don't know what we're going to do."

"You saw me this morning—I was a basket case; I was a wreck. I couldn't bear the fact that you'd left without even saying goodbye."

"You mean, if I'd said goodbye it would have been all right?" Troy asked, in a voice from which he'd removed any emotion.

"No, that's not what I mean at all! I felt as though I'd cut my own throat...as though I was dying because I'd sent you away." Her fingers tightened convulsively round his ribs. "I don't understand anything any more. Least of all me."

She was shivering even more violently, her face a mask of misery. Praying for wisdom, Troy said, "Lucy, I was a damn fool to do what I did this morning, and I'm sorry. I swear I won't ever do anything like that again. I don't have any easy answers for you. I love you—that's all I can say. And I don't even think you want to hear that." He swallowed, trying not to stare at her breasts, at their ripe fullness under her wet T-shirt. "I do think you need some dry clothes, and we both need to get back to the inn as soon as we can—you must be worn out."

"After I saw you, I walked to the cliffs to try and settle down. On the way back there was an egret in the savannah—a white one. It was so beautiful. I was trying to get a closer look at it and I wasn't paying any attention to the weather. All of a sudden the fog was all around me, and I didn't have a clue which way I'd come. I tried to follow my footsteps, but I lost them part-way.'' Lucy rubbed her cheek against his collarbone. "It's really spooky out here—I'm so glad you found me.''

"Not half as glad as I am,'' Troy said. He swung his haversack off his back and pulled out the sweater and the Thermos. "I'll give you my jacket too,'' he added.

She eased her hands free of his body. Her movements slow and deliberate, her eyes trained on his face, she pulled her wet T-shirt over her head and let it fall to the ground. Then she reached for the sweater he was holding out.

It was months since Troy had seen her naked, months since she had lain with him in the act of love. In one swift glance he took in the utter beauty of her breasts, taut-nippled and firm, and the arch of her ribs cradling the concavity of her belly where it disappeared under the waistband of her jeans. He clenched his jaw, so hungry for her that he could feel nothing else. "You're my world,'' he muttered. "My soul circles you... How could it be otherwise?''

She tugged the sweater away from him and gracelessly hauled it over her head. "We can't go on like this— we're killing each other.''

"So what do you suggest we do?'' he said in a raw voice.

"I don't know—I just don't know.''

He pulled off his jacket and put it round her shoulders. Briefly she buried her face in it. Looking up at him, she whispered, "It's warm—it smells of you. Oh, Troy, I can't bear to keep on hurting you!''

"I came here of my own choice,'' Troy said, with a careful lack of emphasis.

"You came here because you couldn't stay away," she replied, with a suppressed violence that produced in him an unsettling mixture of hope and desire.

"That, too," he said with a crooked smile.

Not looking at him, Lucy mumbled, "You'll get cold without your jacket."

"I'll be okay. Here, drink this."

She wrapped her fingers round the plastic mug and gulped the hot coffee. "That feels better."

"We'd better head back—we should let the others know you're safe. Keith and Quentin and the birders are out looking for you as well."

Lucy stood up, pulling his jacket around her. "I've caused a lot of trouble."

"Yeah," said Troy.

She gave him the gamine grin that he'd always loved. "The egret was awfully pretty," she said.

Troy began rewinding the tape, leading the way across the hummocks of bright green grass. At the bridge he leaned back to take Lucy's hand, helping her keep her balance. When she landed with an awkward scramble beside him, he put his arm around her to prevent her from falling. She looked up at him, her eyes still troubled. Then, with the impulsiveness that was so much a part of her character, she pulled his head down and kissed him full on the mouth.

Her lips were damp, and her cold hands on the back of his neck sent chills down Troy's spine. They might be surrounded by fog, he thought, but here, with Lucy, there was only the utmost clarity. And then, as he felt her tongue flick against his lips, he stopped thinking altogether.

She pulled back a few moments later, breathing fast, her cheeks a hectic pink. "My mother always says I act before I think—but sometimes I think too much."

"When I'm within ten feet of you, my thought processes go into reverse," Troy said thickly. "Although I'm darned if we'll make love in a bog, Lucy."

"Make love," she repeated, almost as though she was saying the words for the first time in her life. "I wish I wasn't so afraid—I wish I had even half your certainty!"

"I know you still love me."

"Well, yes—this morning was a dead giveaway as far as that's concerned, wasn't it?" She pulled her wet hair back from her face, giving him a rueful smile. "Not that it's made things any simpler. Less so, if anything."

The skin under her eyes was blue-shadowed. Part of Troy urged him to push her now, while she was tired and vulnerable and might consequently surrender. But if he did so, would they both regret it afterward? Hoping he was making the right decision, he said, "I'm not going to go away, and we don't have to decide anything right now—you look as though you need at least twelve hours of uninterrupted sleep."

"Mmm." She looked around with a reminiscent shudder. "I really don't care if I never see this swamp again."

Troy picked up the roll of tape, from where it had fallen on the ground when Lucy had kissed him, and started off again—and, as was so often the case, the way home didn't seem to take nearly as long as the way out. But it was dusk by the time they reached her cabin.

Troy said, "Hot bath, Lucy—I'll tell them you're found, and I'll bring over some of Mrs Mossop's soup in a few minutes." He added, with an attempt at humor that didn't quite succeed, "And for Pete's sake don't kiss me goodnight, or I won't be answerable for the consequences."

She grimaced. "It's crazy, isn't it? The way I'm behaving, you'd think I was out on my first date instead of married to you... Apologize to Keith and Anna for me, please, Troy? I really am sorry to have caused so much trouble."

As it happened, Keith and the birders had returned only a few minutes before Troy; they were all drinking coffee in the kitchen, along with Anna. As Troy walked in Keith said sharply, "Any luck, Troy?"

Troy explained what had happened and presented Lucy's apologies. "I'm sure she'll thank you in person tomorrow, but she's tired and cold, and I thought she should go straight to bed."

"I'm glad she's all right," said Keith. "A September fog at night is no place to be."

It was the longest sentence Troy had ever heard him say. Anna added, "I'll heat up some soup, Troy, and maybe you could take it over. You tell her I'll do breakfast in the morning; I don't want to see her a minute before eleven."

His throat tight, Troy said, "I want to add my thanks to hers. You both really care about her, don't you?"

"Of course we do," Anna said. "She's become a real friend to me over the last four months. I'd be lost without her."

"Right," said Keith.

"You'd better call Quentin, Keith," Anna said. "He'll be relieved as well."

Lucy hadn't fallen in love with Quentin; Troy knew that now. She'd never fallen out of love with her own husband.

* * *

Fifteen minutes later Troy tapped on the cabin door. Lucy opened it. Her housecoat was belted tightly round her waist and her hair stood out from her face in a cloud of curls. She smelled deliciously of soap and powder and of that indefinable essence that was Lucy, and that Troy would have recognized blindfolded in a roomful of strangers. He said rapidly, thrusting the tray at her, "Anna says you're not to go to work before eleven, and Keith actually produced a dozen words in a row—I think you're forgiven."

She said, holding the tray in front of her like a shield, "Will you stay while I eat this? I'm not—I mean, I'd just like your company."

I'm not inviting you into my bed, was what she was saying. But in Ottawa five months ago she'd scarcely even let him in the door of her apartment. "Sure," said Troy. The alternative was to go back to the kitchen and drink coffee that he didn't need and that would keep him awake all night.

She sat down at the table and took a big bite of Mrs Mossop's homemade bread. Darkness was pressing at the windows, and again Troy had that feeling of being isolated from the rest of the world. But this time, he thought with a dry throat, he was with Lucy. He said, "This morning I gave Clarence a message to fax to the institute in Arizona—I'm not going to take that job, Lucy. In a way, it's got nothing to do with you. I'd be running away if I were to take it—I've worked that out since I got here."

She swallowed a mouthful of soup. Her face very serious, she said, "So you won't be selling the house?"

He shook his head. From nowhere the words tumbled from his mouth. "Lucy, have you ever been unfaithful to me?"

Her spoon stopped in mid-air. ''No,'' she said baldly. ''It's been a long time.''

''Troy, I could get pregnant with someone else just as easily as with you.''

''So is that the only reason you've stayed out of other men's beds?'' he demanded. ''Because you're afraid of getting pregnant?''

''No.'' Her spoon clattered against the plate. ''You're determined to make me say it, aren't you, Troy? All right, I'll say it, then. I still love you—I never stopped loving you—that's why I haven't been unfaithful to you.''

She didn't look particularly loving; rather, she looked cross and belligerent. But Troy believed her instantly, and felt as though a great weight had lifted from his shoulders. Something must have shown in his face because Lucy demanded, ''You thought I'd spent the last year and a half bed-hopping?''

''Hubert made me wonder if you'd been to bed with Quentin.''

''Hubert knows about as much about women as you know about warblers,'' she scoffed, and took a big spoonful of soup.

''The males are bigger, smarter and more colorful than the females,'' Troy said promptly.

In spite of herself Lucy laughed. ''Hubert's a chauvinist. He'd prefer me barefoot and pregnant—that way I'd stay out of trouble.'' She took another mouthful of soup.

How many times had he and Lucy sat at their kitchen table late at night, sharing a snack and talking over the events of the day? And then—Troy's thoughts marched on—going upstairs to lie close together in the middle of their big bed. They hadn't always made love. But there was more to intimacy than making love—it hadn't taken

Troy many weeks of marriage to learn that—and when Lucy had left him it had been simple touch that he'd missed as much as sex. The way she'd used to cuddle into his chest and pull his arm to lie across her breast. The sweet scent of her hair under his chin. The tenderness that had seemed to encase them like a cocoon.

She had never stopped loving him; he knew that now. But he was still far from confident that she would come back home with him. How could he possibly leave her here? Go home alone?

Restlessly he pushed back his chair. "I'm going to get some of that soup for myself," he said. "I'm hungry."

Staring down at the soup, as though the carrots and onions floating on its surface might provide her with answers, Lucy said evenly, "I've been horribly unfair to you the last year, Troy, and I'm truly sorry. But it hasn't been fun for me, either."

"We've got to talk about Michael!" Troy exclaimed, forgetting about caution.

Lucy seemed to shrink inside her housecoat. "Yes. Yes, I guess we do."

It was a huge concession. Forcing himself to sound calm and in control, Troy said, "But not tonight, sweetheart. I'll see you in the morning. After eleven o'clock."

"Goodnight," she muttered, then added in a rush, "I'm so glad it was you who found me."

"Me, too," Troy said, and made his escape.

Lucy still loved him. She had never been unfaithful to him. And she'd agreed to talk to him about their dead son—the one subject that had become taboo during the last few weeks of their marriage. As the fog brushed his face Troy decided he owed it a debt of gratitude. Lucy had been lost. But what had been found filled him with hope and an inexpressible longing.

* * *

At nine-thirty the next morning Troy decided to go and
visit Quentin. He owed the man a vote of thanks for
joining the search yesterday, and—who knew?—maybe
he'd learn something that would be useful in allaying
Lucy's fears.

The fog had cleared, and Hubert's map led Troy to a
small clearing on the western shore, where a cedar-
shingled building that had seen better days leaned into
the winds of the Atlantic. The screen door squealed on
its hinges when he opened it to tap on a wooden door
that could have used a coat of paint. It was apparently
not a painting project that interested Quentin. The door
swung open.

Lucy stood on the threshold.

For a moment Troy was so consumed by an ugly blend
of shock, jealousy and sheer panic that he was struck
dumb. Lucy was gaping at him as if she'd never seen
him before. "What are *you* doing here?" she demanded.

"I could ask the same of you."

"I came to ask Quentin's advice," she said, now
glaring at him rather than gaping.

Belatedly Troy's sense of humor came to his rescue.
"So—more or less—did I," he said, and eased past her
into the room.

A man was standing by the windows that stretched
from floor to ceiling on both the north and west walls
of the house, his back to the light; he was cleaning an
array of brushes on a battered wooden table.

"Good morning," Troy said equably. "I'm Lucy's
husband—Troy Donovan. If I'm startled to find her here
this morning, it's because when I left her cabin last night
she was planning to sleep in."

He was quite openly asserting, one male to another,
his claim to the woman who had closed the door and

plunked herself down in the nearest chair with an air of being very much at home. She gave a rude snort as Quentin wiped his hands on a piece of dirty rag and came over to shake hands.

Quentin's black hair, rather too long, curled over his ears; his eyes were a piercing blue. He was wearing low-slung jeans and a T-shirt that had once been white and was now daubed with streaks and splashes of paint. At some point the sleeves of the shirt had been ripped out, baring an impressive set of muscles. Neither his finger-nails nor his bare feet were as clean as they could have been. While shorter than Troy by a couple of inches, he exuded a blatant masculinity that Troy, as a fellow male, recognized only too well.

Lucy hadn't been unfaithful to him, Troy told himself forcefully. If she'd withstood a man as compelling as Quentin, he, Troy, should congratulate himself.

His eyes sparking with amusement, Quentin said, "I'm very glad—finally—to meet you. Lucy's told me a lot about you."

"Good, bad or indifferent?" Troy asked, with a lift of his brow.

"Rarely indifferent—and I begin to see why. Lucy, why don't you pour your husband a mug of coffee? There are some muffins around somewhere," he finished vaguely.

"There aren't any clean mugs," Lucy announced. "I refuse to wash your dishes for you any more, Quentin."

"Once I finish this canvas, I'll have a cleanup," Quentin said. "Want to see it, Troy? It came out of some of my conversations with Lucy."

He led Troy to the tall easel standing by the window, where the cool northern light fell full on it. With no sense of premonition Troy looked at the painting. His hiss of indrawn breath was totally involuntary; he felt as though someone had, without warning and with diabolical accuracy, hit him hard in the solar plexus. The room fell away, leaving nothing but the bold streaks of black and white on the canvas and the agony of grief that had stabbed him through and through.

A figure—man or woman; it didn't seem to matter—was staring out of a window into what could have been a snowfall. The room surrounding the figure echoed with an emptiness of the spirit that instantly gathered Troy into its cold embrace—an emptiness he had lived with for all too long.

Michael was gone from the room and would never come back.

Michael, his dearly beloved son...

CHAPTER SEVEN

FROM a long distance away Troy became aware that tears lay wet on his cheeks and that his hands were clenched into fists to stop himself from howling his pain out loud like a wild animal. Then he realized something else: Lucy was standing in front of him, putting her body between him and the painting as though to shield him from its impact.

She was clutching his arm, shaking it, her nails digging into his flesh as though to call him back from the place into which he had been thrust. Like a litany she was pleading, "Troy—dearest Troy, don't look like that. I can't bear it. Please, Troy, don't look like that... Quentin, you never should have showed it to him—I didn't know you were going to. Darling Troy, I love you. Oh, please look at me."

A shudder ran through Troy's body. With an actual physical effort he dragged his gaze away from the infinite loneliness of that figure by the window and looked at Lucy. Although there were tears swimming in her eyes, she was holding them back; she looked as fierce as a mother bear defending her cubs, and as frenzied as though she were losing the battle. He swallowed hard and said the first thing that came into his head. "Do you think we'll ever stop missing him?"

She bit her lip. "No," she whispered.

He said, "Sometimes I just go into the nursery and stand there. I seem closer to him, somehow..."

"That's one of the things I ran away from." She raised one hand, and with exquisite gentleness wiped his cheek dry. Then she traced the little network of lines at the corner of his eye. "You've changed in the last year," she said. "You'll always be the most handsome man I've ever seen—that hasn't changed—but you've aged, Troy. You never used to have those gray hairs over your ears; I noticed them the day you arrived here."

All his bitterness at her desertion lay behind Troy's words. "You don't have the corner on suffering, Lucy."

"Grief is so self-centered—so all-absorbing," she cried. "Surely you understand that? It took all my energy just to hold myself together. I didn't have anything left for you—or for anyone else. I see that now, where I didn't—couldn't—at the time." She hesitated. "Troy, what *was* it like for you?"

"You've never asked me that before."

"I'm asking you now," she said.

He spoke without having to think. "The worst time for me was right after you left. At first after he died I did my work automatically... There was kind of an opaque curtain between me and the rest of the world, and through that curtain I operated with total efficiency and no feeling. Everything under control. But once you were gone the curtain dissolved, and it was as if every child I saw was Michael and every parent was myself, and it was up to me to save them all."

He paused, groping to order his thoughts. "I have to have compassion in my job or else I'm nothing but a machine. But I also have to keep a certain objectivity in order to maintain my sanity. Well, I lost my objectivity. All of it. There were no boundaries; there was nowhere to hide. So I drove myself into the ground, trying to save every single child who came into my office."

Lucy looked appalled; from living with him on a day-to-day basis she knew enough about his job to understand some of its terrible pressures.

Troy rubbed at the back of his neck, wishing he hadn't opened this whole subject, and said, "Well, I went to a conference in Washington four or five months after you left and Victor Dillon was there—remember him, the cardiologist who sailed with us on *Seawind*? He took me aside and dragged it all out of me, and read me a lecture about doctors who don't look after themselves, and after that I started to get a sense of proportion back again." He smiled wryly. "Hard work trying to be God— I don't recommend it."

Lucy had always had the talent for going straight to the heart of the matter. She said, "When you needed me, I wasn't there."

Troy could have offered her easy—and untruthful— denials. "No, you weren't," he said.

"How can I ever say I'm sorry? There's no way I can make that up to you!"

"Perhaps you've just started," he said slowly.

She blurted, "Why didn't you stop loving me, Troy?"

"Why does the sun rise? I don't know why, Lucy! God knows, there were times I wanted to. When you left, part of me was relieved, because at least I didn't have to be around you all the time, knowing that I couldn't reach you or help you—that if anything I was making matters worse." His eyes dropped. "Knowing you didn't want to make love any more and yet constantly tormented by your presence."

"That tore me apart—but I couldn't help myself!" She let out her breath in a long sigh. "We haven't been this truthful with each other in months."

"One of the worst things was the way we were so god-damned polite—guarding every word we said so we wouldn't hurt each other more than we'd already been hurt. Like a couple of strangers who'd been thrown together in the same house."

With a faint smile Lucy said, "We've been anything but polite since you got here."

"A distinct improvement." Troy's own smile broke through. "Was I dreaming a little while ago? Or were you tossing around words like 'dearest' and 'darling'?"

As Lucy blushed a kettle screamed a warning behind them. Troy looked around; he had completely forgotten about Quentin. The other man was filling an ultra-modern coffee-machine with boiling water. There was a bowl full of suds in the sink and at least two dozen mugs piled to dry on the rack. Troy said with genuine curiosity, "How often do you wash dishes, Quentin?"

"When I run out of clean ones. Or when things start to smell a bit high. Whichever comes first."

"I brought fresh milk with me this morning," Lucy said. "It's called self-preservation."

"So what were you going to ask Quentin's advice about, Lucy?"

"What I should or shouldn't do next."

"We seem to have solved that on our own."

With a violence that entranced him she said, "I'm *sorry* it's taken me so long to ask you what it was like for you, Troy. I know I withdrew from you... I didn't do it consciously—I swear I didn't."

"It was a bad time for both of us," Troy said, knowing he was speaking the simple truth. "We did the best we could, and sometimes that wasn't enough."

"I do love you," Lucy said vehemently.

"Coffee, anyone?" Quentin asked.

Needing to shake off all the emotions he'd gone through in the last few minutes, Troy seized Lucy round the waist, lifted her off her feet and whirled her around in the air. When he put her back down, he kissed her very explicitly on the mouth, making no attempt to hide the pleasure he took in this. Then he said, "Yeah, I could do with a coffee. Did you find the muffins?"

Quentin chuckled. "I'd stashed them behind the turpentine. No guarantee what they'll taste like."

"I'll risk it," Troy said. "All of a sudden I've got the appetite of a horse."

In exactly the same tone of voice Quentin went on, "I never put the make on Lucy, Troy. Not because she isn't a gorgeous woman and a thoroughly nice one into the bargain—a combination that's not all that thick on the ground—but it was quite clear to me from the start that she wasn't the slightest bit interested in me. Didn't take me long to find out you were the one she was all wrapped up in."

He sloshed milk in his mug and dug at the brown sugar, which had hardened to a rock-like consistency. "I always forget to put the lid on the jar," he said peevishly. "Where was I? Oh, yes, Lucy... She's really stayed the course with Anna. She could've left the minute she got here and found out Anna was pregnant. You hang in there, fella—I guess that's the only advice I'm capable of handing out."

In total exasperation Lucy said, "If you've quite finished discussing me as though I'm nothing but a—a tube of paint——"

"Vermilion," Quentin put in, openly laughing at her.

Ignoring him, she cried, "That's the awful part about it—I don't want anyone else but Troy, and yet I'm too scared to be with him. It's like a war going on inside me all the time. I thought if I came to a new place and called myself Lucy Barnes and took off my wedding-ring, I'd feel different. Free, maybe. Huh! It didn't do a damn thing for me; I still dreamed about Troy every night of the week.''

Lucy rarely swore. Lightheaded from too much emotion, Troy said, "Anytime you want to act on those dreams, I'm available.''

"Oh, right on.'' She scowled at him. "I need a muffin.''

Obligingly Troy passed her one, lightly running his fingers across the curve of her palm as he did so; it had been their private signal in a roomful of people that they would much prefer to be home in bed.

Lucy's blush was indeed very close to vermilion. Quentin turned his laugh into a cough and Troy said, "I'm flattered, by the way, Lucy—I'm quite sure most women would have thrown themselves at Quentin.''

Lucy's scowl deepened. "I love my two sisters, but I've always had a hankering for a brother—and that's how I see Quentin.''

Quentin threw back his head with a whoop of glee. "I knew when I turned thirty-five it would be downhill all the way. Sex appeal zapped, body going to pot, ego in smithereens... Oh, Lucy, I'd be delighted to be your brother.''

Her hands on her hips, Lucy looked from one to the other of the two men. "I will never, if I live to be a hundred, understand the male of the species,'' she declaimed. "I've got to be at work in half an hour. Eat your muffin, Troy.''

"Yes, ma'am,'' Troy said, and watched laughter glint in the gray depths of her eyes. He wasn't out of the woods yet, but he was damned close.

While his muffin did have a whiff of turpentine about it, it tasted very satisfactorily of apple and spices. The coffee was rich and dark. They talked about Quentin's last show in Toronto, and about the barred owl he had heard in the pine trees last night, and as Troy drained his mug and stood up, Quentin said, "Come on over any time, Troy. If I'm working I hang a sign on the door—otherwise you'd be very welcome."

Lucy said darkly, "I'm not sure I want you two getting together—I'm in enough trouble as it is."

But Troy liked Quentin, especially now it was clear that the other man wasn't in any way a rival for Lucy's affections. "I'll do that," he said. "Ready, Lucy?"

He followed her out of the door, and as they came to the beginning of the path he took her by the hand. Her footsteps faltered. Looking up at him, she muttered, "I remember everything about you. In bed and out. And yet at the same time you're like a stranger to me. It's nuts."

Troy brought her hand to his mouth, nuzzling her fingers, then cupped the back of her hand in his palm and kissed her parted lips. Her hair seemed to crackle with energy under his fingertips. With his free hand he found the rise of her breast under her sweater. Stroking it hypnotically, he murmured, "Same man you slept with for three and a half years. Same old technique, my darling."

"It's not funny!" Her eyes wild, her face convulsed with longing, she pressed her hips into his body, into all his throbbing, pent-up need for her. "I missed you so much, Troy," she said brokenly. "But——"

"No buts." He ran his hands down the curve of her spine. "I could make love with you right here on the ground."

"In full view of Quentin?" She leaned away from him. "And I really mustn't be late for work."

Cool it—was that the message? "What time do you get off?" Troy asked as she swung along the trail ahead of him, moving with leggy grace.

"Around two."

"We could go and visit Hubert," he said with low cunning.

"And then the only ones you'd have to kiss me in front of would be Anna and Keith?" Lucy retorted ungrammatically. "I'm on to you, Troy Donovan. Compromise me in front of as many people as you can—that's your plan."

"You're as clever as you are beautiful," he answered agreeably.

"Just for your information, Keith's gone to the mainland for a couple of days. So you'll have to wait." She wrinkled her nose. "As for Hubert, having been a bachelor all his life, he thinks he knows everything there is to know about marriage. Nor is he shy about sharing his opinions. We could pick raspberries by the big pond instead."

Troy didn't care what he did as long he was with Lucy. He delivered her to the back door of the inn, watched her hover indecisively on the step, then felt her pull his head down to kiss him. It wasn't a subtle kiss; it left no doubt in his mind that Lucy wanted him. Detaching herself, she gritted, "I must be stark raving mad," and slammed the door behind her.

Troy went upstairs and had a cold shower.

When Troy presented himself at the back door again at five to two, Lucy was waiting for him. "I can't get off," she said bluntly. "Anna's really tired and I can't leave her to clean the bathrooms on her own—Mrs Mossop's niece went back with Keith. But I'll be through in the kitchen by eight if I hurry. Then we could go down to the beach.''

Eight o'clock was six hours away. "Are you disappointed or relieved?" Troy asked, equally bluntly.

Her eyes dropped. "We've got a lot of talking to do before we do anything...silly."

He was beginning to get angry. "Make love, you mean."

"We've been apart for months—a little longer won't hurt! We have to talk, Troy."

His head agreed with her; his hormones didn't. "Yeah," he said stonily. "I'll see you at dinner."

He went for a long swim that afternoon, thrashing through the water in an effort to tire himself out. By the time he'd waded back to the beach and picked up his towel from the sand, Troy had worked out what was wrong.

Lucy was right. They did need to talk. He had been the one to insist on that. The trouble was, he was still afraid. He wanted to make love to Lucy first and talk afterward. Because only by putting his seal on her in this most intimate and primitive of ways would he really begin to believe that she was going to come back to him.

He scrubbed himself dry, threw his towel over his shoulder and headed back to the inn. As he crossed the upstairs hall to his room Lucy was just backing out of the big closet where the cleaning supplies were kept. She had a toilet brush in one hand and a bottle of disinfectant in the other.

"Hello, Lucy," he said.

The toilet brush fell from her fingers and skittered across the floor. She turned around, her eyes raking the length of his body from his wet hair to his bare feet. Swallowing, she said weakly, "You've been swimming. How was the water?"

He padded over to her and stooped to pick up the toilet brush. Before he could straighten, he felt her hand dart out to touch his shoulder, then as quickly snatch itself away. He got to his feet, passing her the brush. "Cold," he said. "Good for the heart muscles, bad for the libido."

"It'd take the Antarctic to settle me down."

Very pleased by this reply, Troy said, "I'll do my best to rout up a penguin or two... How's Anna?"

"I sent her off to have a rest—she's still tired."

"To paraphrase Quentin, you're both gorgeous and nice." He patted her on the rump. "Back to work."

She was clutching the bottle of disinfectant to her chest like a shield. "Yes," she gasped, and fled across the hall to the nearest bedroom.

She didn't need a toilet brush to clean a bedroom. Much heartened, Troy went to have his second shower of the day.

The beach at eight-thirty that evening was not the setting for romance. The wind had come up, chasing thin-edged clouds across the face of the moon, and waves dashed on the sand and retreated, in an angry, unceasing hiss of spray. The trees, black against the sky, sighed and complained, their branches slapping at each other, the leaves of the alders rattling with every gust.

After she'd finished work, Lucy had showered in her cabin and met Troy on the porch; she had not invited him in. He zippered his jacket, feeling the wind tug his hair. The last thing they'd be doing tonight was making love on the beach, he thought edgily. He wasn't even sure he'd be able to hear himself think.

"There's a driftwood log at the far end of the sand," Lucy called. "We could sit there."

He crossed the ridge, where the shadows cast by the moon writhed on the gray rocks. Back at the inn, the birders had taken over the lounge and the fireplace. Lucy, he was quite sure, wouldn't come to his bedroom, and hers was off-limits. Sunk in his own thoughts, not watching where he was going, Troy tripped over a sharp-edged chunk of granite, grabbed at the log for support and gave a grunt of pain.

Lucy whirled to face him. "What's wrong?"

He was cradling his right hand in his left. She came closer, pried his hand away and said, "Oh, Troy, how did you do that?"

"Pull it out, will you?"

A jagged splinter, at least half an inch long, had embedded itself in the flesh at the base of his thumb. She said, obviously upset, "I can't do it in the dark—we'll have to go back to the cabin. I've got a little first-aid kit there I use for hiking. Does it hurt?"

"Yeah...they always say doctors make the worst patients."

She tugged at his sleeve. "Come on, you're bleeding."

Back at the cabin, they left their shoes at the door, Troy awkwardly unlacing his with one hand. It only took Lucy a few moments to light three kerosene lamps and place them close together on the table. After rummaging around in her little bathroom, she produced tweezers, peroxide and a small roll of bandage.

Troy had shrugged out of his jacket. She pulled her sweater over her head, revealing a tailored sage-green shirt whose severity, in Troy's eyes, merely emphasized the tumbled mass of her curls and the softness of her lips. His mouth dry, he pulled out a chair. Lucy washed her hands in the sink and sat down beside him.

"I'll be as gentle as I can," she said, and took his hand in hers.

For what was really a very minor injury, the pain was disproportionate. Troy concentrated on the delicacy of Lucy's touch, on the way she was chewing her lower lip as she probed at the wound to get out all the slivers of wood. The lamplight shone on her cheek and traced the bump in her nose that gave her face some of its character; he could even see the little flecks of color in her irises beneath their fringe of dark lashes.

She glanced up and said in distress, "I'm sorry I'm hurting you, Troy—it's nearly all out."

The deepest fragment hurt the most. As she triumphantly waved it in front of his nose, he let out his breath. "Douse my hand with peroxide," he said, then couldn't help flinching when she did so.

Not looking at him, she daubed on some ointment and tied a neat bandage around the base of his thumb. "There," she said in a strained voice, "it's done."

"Lucy——"

Troy was never sure afterward if he pulled Lucy to her feet or if she stood up at the same time as he. He did remember that one of the chairs crashed to the floor and that neither of them paid it the least attention. She fell into his arms even as he reached for her, their mouths meeting in a kiss so hungry that it obliterated everything else in the room except the woman who was clinging to him as if she never wanted to let him go. With an inarticulate groan Troy picked her up. She laced her hands around his neck, her eyes burning into his.

He kissed her again, loving her weight, the dig of her spine into his elbow, all the warmth and passion that was Lucy. There was only one place to go, and he had never been more sure in his life that he was doing the right thing—the only thing possible. Walking over to the bed, he laid her down on the blue coverlet.

Drinking in her beauty, he stood over her for a moment. How long since he had seen her hair spread in a rich cloud over her pillow? Too long. All those aching months of loneliness too long. And how long since he had lain beside her?

He fell on to the bed, wrapping his arms around her and straining her to his body, his face buried in the tangled mass of her hair. Throwing one leg over her thighs, he found her mouth again, and was offered the same ardent welcome. She was tugging at the buttons on his shirt, kissing him, whimpering his name, and he let the last of the barriers fall to the ground. He had no need of them. Lucy, his beloved Lucy, was his again.

Her hands slid across his bare chest, tugging at the blond hair that curled to his navel. He yanked his shirt out of his waistband, flinging it to one side, and heard her whisper, "Oh, Troy, how beautiful you are—I've missed you so much."

Resting on one elbow, he traced the dark wings of her brows and the jut of her cheekbones, then kissed the softness of her mouth with a lingering sensuality that inflamed every cell in his body. His hand moved lower, unbuttoning her shirt and pushing it back so he could rest his face on the smooth rise of her breast.

She gasped, "I feel as though I've never made love in my life before—I want you so much." Her fingertips fluttered over the hard muscles of his shoulders and the scar on his ribs in a journey of rediscovery that shot through all Troy's nerve-endings. Then she fumbled at his belt. "I want to feel you all over," she whispered. "Please, Troy...love me as you've never loved me before."

Troy was almost afraid he was dreaming, so often had he longed to hear her say such words. Sitting up, he drew her up beside him and unbuttoned the rest of her shirt, easing it from her shoulders. In the lamplight they were a creamy gold. Running his palms down their gentle slope, he reached for the catch on her bra and pulled that free of her body as well. Then he bent to her breasts, cupping their fullness in his hands, sliding his lips to each rose-pink tip.

Lucy was moaning with pleasure, her head thrown back, her fingers caught in his hair. He could feel her fierce impatience, for it matched his own; with all his will power he set out to prolong the exquisite pleasure of a mating as elemental as the voices of wind and sea.

Later, he was to wonder if Lucy had caught his mood. For, with an eroticism that made the blood pound in his ears, she brushed her breasts against the hard wall of his chest, her arms all sinuous curves, her eyes like dark pools. Undoing his belt, she slid the zipper down on his jeans; a pang shot through him as he felt her hands on his erection.

He said, his voice sounding almost like an intrusion over his heightening breathing, "Two can play that game, my love," and began tugging her jeans down her hips.

"Indeed, they can," she replied, with the gamine grin that had always melted his heart, and in a flurry of bare legs tossed her jeans to the floor.

Without finesse Troy hauled the rest of his clothes from his body and kicked them to one side. "I want to see you naked," he whispered, and lifted her hips to remove the scrap of pale green lace from between her legs. Then he let his hand rest on the softness of her belly, where stretchmarks had left a visible memento of their son.

He didn't want to think about Michael. Not now. Now was for Lucy, and for her alone.

Almost roughly he parted her thighs, and to his wonderment and infinite gratification found that she was wet and warm and waiting. "Lucy," he said huskily, "dearest Lucy..."

She clasped his waist, pulling him down on top of her so he could feel the heat of her body all the way from his shoulders to his knees. With an instinct he couldn't have gainsaid Troy thrust into her; she opened for him, and for a moment that was enough, simply to be held by her. "I've come home," he said hoarsely. "Where I belong. There's nowhere else I want to be—ever."

The demands of his body were overwhelming him. He fought against them, withdrawing from her and hearing her tiny sound of protest. He rolled over and pulled her on top of him. The valley between her breasts was deeply shadowed, her hair falling forward over her face. Her features blurred with tenderness, Lucy took him in her hands again, playing with him until his face convulsed, and only then raising her hips so she could ride him as a petrel rode the waves.

This had long been one of their favorite ways to make love. As if there had been no intervening months when he had been without her, Troy's fingers found the place where she was most sensitive to his touch; her skin was as sleek as the pelt of a seal and her indrawn breath like a sob. His gaze trained to her face, Troy watched her spiral deeper and deeper into rhythms as old as time. She arched her body over his, her hands pressed to his pelvis, and with all his strength he thrust into her, again and again.

Heat and darkness and color, swirling into a vortex that was sucking him ever deeper ... He saw her break, felt the inner pulsing where she held him so intimately, and finally let go himself. Even as a harsh groan burst from his lips Lucy collapsed on top of him; they lay still, bodies entwined.

Troy said breathlessly, "I love you, Lucy. I love you so much."

"I love you, too."

He clasped her in his arms, marveling as always at the silky smoothness of her skin. "I can feel your heartbeat."

"And I yours," she said contentedly.

"Maybe we should get under the covers—I don't want you to get cold."

"I don't want to move. Not yet. This feels too nice."

She was nuzzling into his chest in a way that disarmed him. He stroked her hair and said with a thread of laughter, "I forgot all about my sore hand."

"I should hope so."

Utterly happy, Troy closed his eyes, idly playing with her hair. "I'll show a little more finesse next time," he said. "Wouldn't want you to have cause to complain."

She rested her chin on his breastbone, openly laughing at him. "When have you ever known me to complain?"

"There was that one time I'd been in the OR for over twelve hours and I kept falling asleep."

"But don't you remember the next morning? You more than made up for it."

He did remember. "Weren't we rolling around on the living-room carpet and your sister Marcia came to call?"

Lucy giggled. "I've never dressed so fast in my whole life. And then after she left I discovered I had my blouse on backward—I'm sure she knew exactly what we'd been up to." Planting a row of kisses along his collarbone, she added thoughtfully, "I've never understood Marcia. She's so beautiful—much more so than me or Catherine—and yet I don't think she'll ever get married."

"I object," Troy growled. "I married the most beautiful of the Barnes sisters. And this isn't the time to discuss Marcia's love-life. Or lack of it."

Lucy was nibbling at his skin now, her cheek lying over his heart, and because he felt safe and happy and invulnerable it didn't occur to him to censor his words. "If you keep that up, Lucille Elizabeth, you're going to get into trouble," he said. "We always figured that morning on the carpet was when Michael got started, didn't we?"

Lucy's whole body froze. When she raised her face it was chalk-white, and Troy cursed himself for being so insensitive. "I'm sorry," he said. "We'll have lots of time to talk about Michael later on."

She rolled off him and sat up with none of her usual grace; she looked distraught.

Leaning on one elbow, trying to keep the anger from his voice, Troy said, "Lucy, I'm not going to apologize every time I mention his name."

Wanting her beside him again, certain that his touch could calm her, he reached out for her. She pushed him away and said in a cracked voice, "I could be pregnant right now. Because of what we just did."

He frowned. "The odds of that when you're on the pill are almost nil—you mustn't worry so."

"I stopped taking any pills after I moved to Ottawa."

"You *what*?"

"You heard. I didn't need them; I wasn't going to bed with anyone. I—just stopped thinking about them. They weren't important. That's why I didn't think about them now." She closed her eyes. "I'm in the riskiest part of my cycle—how could I have been so *stupid*?"

Troy sat up. "I don't think you were being stupid at all," he said. "It's very simple. You made love to me because you wanted to. Because you love——"

"I let myself be sweet-talked into it," she said wildly. "You knew that was my greatest fear, Troy—all along you've known it. How *could* you have taken me to bed?"

"I didn't know you weren't protected against a pregnancy because you didn't tell me," he said levelly. "And I took you to bed because that's where both of us wanted to be, and we do happen to be married."

"We're separated!" she spat.

The word struck him to the heart. "Don't, Lucy, for God's sake."

"It's true! I've never agreed to move back in with you."

Troy fought to keep his temper; because below it, like the sunken part of an iceberg, lay a paralyzing fear. "Will you please calm down? The last few days we've moved well beyond the stage of trading insults. And if by chance you are pregnant—the odds are against it, cycle or no cycle—I for one would be very happy."

Lucy was staring at him with as much hostility as if he were an enemy. Her own worst enemy. "I don't want another child."

"I agree we've got a lot to sort out before——"

"You're not listening to me! It was totally irresponsible of me to forget I wasn't taking anything—I can't believe I was such a fool. I should never have made love with you—never. I regret that I ever——" Her eyes suddenly widened. "Did you get that splinter on purpose? So we'd come back here? So you could seduce me?"

With a distant part of his mind Troy thought how funny it was that a few words could so easily smash happiness into the small shards that sliced into him like splinters of glass. Glass, not wood. He got up from the bed and reached for his clothes, pulling them on without paying them the least attention. "If you had to do it over again," he said, spacing each word with cold precision, "you wouldn't go to bed with me?"

"Of course not! That's what I've been trying to tell you. I can't imagine why you even have to ask that question."

Through an immense lethargy, different in quality from any tiredness his work had ever caused him, Troy struggled with the buttons on his shirt. "I can't take this any more, Lucy," he said. "I can't detach my body— my sexuality—from my love for you—they're inextricable. They're part of me. Part of us. But you don't want to make love with me. You want guarantees that you'll never be hurt again—cast-iron guarantees—and I can't give them to you. It's beyond my power."

He looked around for his shoes. The words he had just spoken seemed totally inadequate to express the place into which her words had cast him—a place all the more bleak because of the intimacy they'd just shared. A place of darkness where he was all alone again.

He should never have come to the island. Certainly he shouldn't have made love with Lucy. All the old wounds had been reopened, and he had no one but himself to blame.

His shoes were by the door. He said, "I'll radio Clarence in the morning and go home."

Lucy—noticeably—did not reply.

On his way to the door Troy almost stumbled over a chair. Remembering how it had toppled to the floor, he felt a shaft of pain lance his chest like the stab of a knife. Shoving his feet in his shoes, he opened the door. The moon shadows lay cold and crisp on the grass. He said, not looking at Lucy, "Should you be pregnant, get in touch with me—you know where I am. Otherwise I'll file for a divorce. Because if you've been a fool, so have I. It's time I learned to let go of something that's been dead for months."

He closed the door behind him and stepped off the porch; his feet felt detached from the rest of his body, so that he had to concentrate on placing one in front of the other. Like a child learning to walk, he thought.

He had lost.

The relentless sound of the sea filled his ears, and passionately he wished that he could get on a boat this very minute.

He'd go tomorrow.

And he wouldn't come back.

CHAPTER EIGHT

THE clouds had blown away from the moon so that its cold and perfect circle shone full in Troy's face. Tripping over the rough ground, he headed for the beach. The wind had lessened. He'd leave Shag Island tomorrow even if he had to swim for it, he decided grimly, and through the trees caught his first glimpse of the pale sand.

The moonlight was trembling on the water; foam flared from the crests of the waves, whose troughs shone like obsidian. It was a composition in black and white, starkly beautiful. Worthy of Quentin, Troy thought, and felt vaguely sorry that he'd never see Quentin again.

He stared blankly at the waves, immune both to their beauty and their indifference. I've got to go home, he told himself. I've got to forget everything that happened here.

The wind was cold. He did up his jacket, and as he reached for the tab under his chin he caught the elusive scent of Lucy's body from his hands. Shoving them in his pockets, he fought back emotions that if he allowed them space would drown him as surely as the black waves could pull him beneath the sea.

Enough of emotion. He was leaving here. Leaving Lucy.

Somehow he had to learn to live without her.

When he next looked up the moon had climbed appreciably higher in the sky, and his watch informed him it was nearly one-thirty. He climbed the bank, his movements stiff and awkward because he was chilled through and through. If he could make it until dawn he'd be all right. Once he was on a plane, heading west, he'd get his sense of proportion back.

He'd have to. He had no choice.

Lucy's cabin was in darkness. Troy walked past it and crossed the deck of the inn, opening the door that led into the living-room. It was—not to his surprise—empty. But as he stepped into the hallway, where the stairs led to his bedroom, he saw a swath of light angling across the gleaming hardwood from the rooms where Keith and Anna lived.

He didn't want to talk to anyone. He just wanted to be alone. He walked down the hall and called softly, "Anna? Are you all right? Did Keith get back?"

"Troy?" she faltered. "Is that you?"

"Can I come in?"

"Please...I've been looking for you."

He had never been in their living-room before. He got a quick impression of books everywhere and of richly colored crewel embroidery that far surpassed any of Lucy's efforts. There was light shining from another door, the door to a bedroom whose pristine white curtains and duvet were again enlivened by the ruby reds and aquamarines of Anna's needlework.

Anna was leaning against the wall. She was wearing a long white nightgown, her black hair loose on her shoulders. Troy said, "You're in labor."

"My water broke an hour ago and the contractions are about eight minutes apart," she said, giving him an unhappy smile. "Bad timing... I was a week late with Stephen so I guess I was counting on that this time. Not two weeks early with——" her lip quivered "—Keith away."

Troy gave her his most reassuring smile. "You'll have to put up with me instead. Who else is around?"

"No one." Her eyes widened, her attention turning inward as she breathed hard through a contraction. Glancing at her watch, she said, "Seven minutes . . . The birders are out with the petrels, and I couldn't find you. I was trying to get up the energy to walk over to Lucy's cabin when I heard you. I'm *very* glad to see you." She began walking back and forth by the bed, carrying the burden of her child with the dignity Troy had noticed before in women at full term, her hands pressed into the small of her back. "Will you go and get Lucy, Troy?"

"Where's Mrs Mossop?" he answered evasively.

"I don't want Mrs Mossop. For one thing she has a stock of old wives' tales that would curl your hair, for another she passes out at the sight of blood. Mrs Mossop in a faint on my bedroom floor wouldn't be helpful."

"Oh," said Troy.

"I know Lucy won't want to come," Anna said. "But I need her. I really do—tell her that, will you?" She pulled a face. "And tell her to hurry."

He really had no other choice. He'd need help, and Lucy was the obvious and only option. Great, Troy thought. The grand denunciation scene and three hours later I'm knocking on her door. "I'll be right back," he said.

He hurried outside and crossed the grass to Lucy's cabin. Taking a deep breath, he raised his fist and rapped on the door.

"Who's there?"

She hadn't been asleep or she couldn't have answered so quickly. "It's Troy. Anna's in labor."

The door was thrown open. Lucy's face was pale, her hair in a wild cloud around her face. "She's not due yet," Lucy said.

"Just in case you're accusing me of another trick," Troy snarled, "her contractions are seven minutes apart and she needs you. Come as quickly as you can, will you?"

"I can't," Lucy said in a stifled voice. "Troy, I can't."

"You can and you will."

Her face crumpled. "I can't watch a baby being born; that's asking too much of me."

"Lucy," Troy said with icy precision. "Keith's on the mainland, Mrs Mossop faints at the sight of blood, Stephen's nine years old and the birders are crashing around in the woods. There's no one else. Have you got that? No one else."

"I don't care! I'm not going!"

"Anna asked for you. She needs you."

"I can't go," Lucy repeated helplessly. "I just can't."

Quite rationally, Troy decided to lose his temper. Not bothering to keep his voice down, not caring who heard him, he seethed, "I've had enough of your histrionics, Lucy! More than enough. I'm sick to death of listening to you complain about how afraid you are of anything that might touch your precious emotions."

"That's——"

"Fathers grieve, too—I thought you'd gotten that message at Quentin's. But I had to get on with it. I had a job, and a wife I loved, and a marriage I cared about—and I did the best I could with all three. But oh, no, that wasn't good enough for you."

He paused for breath. Now that he'd started, feelings held in check for over a year were thundering through him like a cavalry charge, and the stricken look on Lucy's face only served to spur him on.

"You shut yourself off from me," he accused her. "You wouldn't talk to me about Michael, you'd scarcely cry in front of me—and you certainly never offered me any comfort. Instead you ran away to Ottawa, back to your mother and your sisters, because there wasn't a chance that they'd challenge you to change—they all keep their emotions ever so nicely in check. You knew you'd be safe there."

His eyes narrowed. "As far as I'm concerned, you can keep on running, Lucy—I don't give a sweet goddamn what you do any more! You can hide from reality for the rest of your life." He seized her by the arm. "But right now you're coming over to help Anna give birth to her child. You're not being offered a choice. You'll come if I have to throw you over my shoulder and carry you—do you hear me?"

He was yelling, he realized. Quentin and Hubert had probably heard him. But he wasn't going to retract one word. Not one single word. "You know what?" he added, into a silence that Lucy didn't seem about to break. "I feel ten pounds lighter. Past time I said all that."

Lucy's face was blank with shock. She must have been crying before he knocked on her door; her nose was still pink and her eyelids swollen. Good, Troy thought trenchantly, and realized something else. She was wearing the same clothes she'd taken off for their love-making. So she hadn't gone to sleep at all after he'd left.

Not that he cared. He said impatiently, "I've got to get back to Anna—are you coming on your own or do I have to drag you over there?"

"You've changed," Lucy faltered. "You never used to be so hard. So uncompromising."

"If I am, it's because you've made me so."

She winced. "I'll be over in a minute. I've got to wash my face first."

"Hurry up, then," he said curtly, turned on his heel and ran back to the inn.

For a man who'd undoubtedly just destroyed any lingering hope that his wife would ever come back to him, he was feeling remarkably good. He hurried through the living-room and the hall and into Anna's apartment. Anna was leaning against the wall of her bedroom, panting. When the contraction had loosened its hold, he said, "Lucy'll be right over. I'll fix the bed, Anna, so you've got somewhere to lie down when you need a rest."

She gave him a relieved smile. "Glad you're back... I'm best to keep moving at this stage."

Troy took off the duvet and the embroidered pillows, and puffed up the remaining pillows. Then he found a stash of clean towels and, under Anna's directions, got out the tiny garments the baby would need. Finally he checked Anna's progress. While the baby was perfectly placed, it looked as though they could be in for an all-night session.

Anna said diffidently, "I hope Lucy didn't mind—did she?"

"Of course not," Troy lied. "Isn't that her coming?"

A moment or two later Lucy took off her shoes at the door, then kissed Anna on the cheek. "How are you getting along?"

"I'm so glad you're here," Anna said. "I know this probably isn't easy for you."

"It's just fine," Lucy said. "I'm glad I can help."

She sounded as though she meant every word, and Troy had to look closely to see that she had been crying. Inwardly applauding her, he said, "I'm going to put some water on to boil in the kitchen, Lucy."

When he came back Lucy was massaging the small of Anna's back between the contractions, which were stronger and more frequent. There was little for Troy to do at this point. He sat down in the rocking chair in the corner of the room, watching the two women in the warm glow of the lamplight. Lucy might not want to be here. But she was supporting Anna wholeheartedly, in a way he couldn't fault.

She was showing the courage he'd thought had deserted her.

The courage he'd accused her of losing.

He remembered unbuttoning her shirt and burying his face in the softness of her breasts, and got to his feet restively, going into the kitchen to check that he'd done everything he should have. As he stared through the window at the silvered woods he could admit to himself that, ironically, he was dreading this birth almost as much as Lucy.

He paced up and down the kitchen floor. He checked Anna again. When the birders clumped into the living-room he told them what was going on, and had to smile when they scuttled upstairs as fast as they could. Rather like a flock of sandpipers, he thought, and paced some more.

He was standing by the window when Lucy came in the kitchen. She said, "You look like you need a massage more than Anna."

Troy didn't want Lucy seeing the tension in his shoulders, or guessing his own fears about the birth of

Anna's child. "No, thanks," he said briefly. "How's she doing?"

"Every four minutes." Clear-eyed, her feet planted squarely on the floor, Lucy went on, "I truly am glad to be here, Troy; it's no act. What you said really shook me up."

It was the old Lucy, who had always owned her faults and been as honest with him as with herself. But the old Lucy had loved being in bed with him, had loved everything they did there. This Lucy didn't. "I'd better take another look at Anna," Troy said.

At a little after four in the morning Anna's contractions intensified. "This is the hardest time," Troy said gently, watching anxiety pool in her eyes as she gripped his hand with bruising strength. "Yell, sing, swear—do whatever you have to do. Just don't bear down—not yet."

Lucy was on Anna's other side; they were working very much as a team, he thought, and remembered how Lucy at this stage had shouted nursery rhymes at the top of her lungs, to the disconcertion of the young resident in Obstetrics who had been attending her. Lucy had never been one to do things by half measures.

About twenty minutes later Troy said, "Okay, now's the time to push, Anna. Take a deep breath when the contraction begins and bear down as hard as you can when it peaks. You're doing just fine."

Her face was streaked with sweat and her eyes huge. As Lucy wiped her forehead Anna puffed, "Remind me when this is over never to do it again, will you?" Then she gathered all her energy for the next contraction.

She worked valiantly and hard, and exactly thirty-four minutes after Troy had spoken the baby's head and shoulders were out and the rest of her body followed.

It was a girl—a whole and healthy child, Troy saw, and he said to Lucy, "Hold her for me while I wipe her eyes and nose, will you?"

For a moment he thought Lucy was going to refuse. Her face was a study in conflicting emotions; she could as easily have laughed for joy or burst into hysterical tears. The baby gave a gasping cry and opened eyes that were the dark purple of pansies. They fastened themselves on Lucy's face, then blinked once, twice. Sheer wonderment eclipsed all the rest of Lucy's feelings. Looking as though she had just witnessed a miracle, she took the slippery bundle from him.

"A lovely, healthy little girl," he said to Anna, examining the baby from head to foot, his hands swift and sure and very gentle. "Lucy, why don't you put the baby on Anna's belly? It'll help with the last few contractions."

With infinite care, Lucy did as he asked. He saw the glow of awe and love on Anna's exhausted face, the tears in Lucy's eyes, and felt an upsurge of gratitude that everything had gone well. Without fuss, he cut the cord and delivered the placenta. Then he cleaned up in the kitchen and brought in warm water to bathe the baby.

Lucy did this, with a tenderness that made Troy's heart ache. Wrapping the infant in a soft blanket, she put her on Anna's breast, her hands lingering, as though reluctant to give up their burden. Then she mumbled, "I'd like a cup of tea. Shall I make you one, too, Troy?"

"If you're not offering champagne, tea'd be fine," he said, grinning at her.

She was staring at him as if she'd never seen him before. "If I'd been Anna, I'd have had complete trust in you," she blurted.

Anna said with a radiant smile, "Lucy's absolutely right, Troy. You're so calm and competent—quite a guy!

Thank you, too, Lucy. I'll never forget how you and Troy were here when I needed you.''

''I'm going to be blubbering like a baby myself in a minute,'' Lucy muttered, and fled to the kitchen.

While Troy set up the cradle by the bed Anna phoned Keith. ''He really wanted a little girl,'' she said happily as she turned off the cellular phone. ''He'll be home as soon as he can—Clarence will bring him—and he's so grateful to the two of you for being here with me.''

The birth of his daughter had made Keith positively loquacious, Troy thought wryly, helping himself to the cookies Lucy was offering him. They all drank tea and ate oatmeal bars as the first light of dawn peeked through the cracks in the curtains. Then Lucy glanced at her watch and yelped, ''I have to have breakfast ready and four lunches packed in three-quarters of an hour—the birders are going to the cliffs, so they want to make an early start.''

''Maybe Troy'll lend you a hand,'' Anna said sleepily. ''That way he can keep an eye on me and the baby until Keith comes. Is that okay with you, Troy?''

Now that Keith was returning to the island today, Troy could go back to the mainland with Clarence. It would work out perfectly. Telling himself that the heaviness in his chest was from eating too many oatmeal bars, Troy said, ''Sure. I'm leaving today, Anna, so I'll be able to travel with Clarence.''

''Leaving?'' Anna said in dismay, looking from him to Lucy. ''I thought——''

From an obscure need to protect Lucy, Troy said, ''I have to get back to work. I've stayed here longer than I intended as it is.''

''Oh,'' said Anna. ''I do hope I'll see both of you again next summer.''

He managed a credible smile. "You never know. Lucy, what do you want me to do in the kitchen?"

"You can make the fruit salad while I get the muffins in the oven," she said, not looking at him.

So five minutes later Troy was slicing oranges and dicing pears in the kitchen while Lucy beat eggs and sugar together on the other side of the counter. Troy could think of nothing to say that he hadn't already said; Lucy also seemed disinclined to talk, plying her wooden spoon with ferocious energy.

When he'd chopped enough fruit, he added raisins and coconut to the salad and put it on the dining-room table. He then began frying large quantities of bacon on the stove. The muffins smelled delicious, as did the coffee brewing in the Pyrex pot.

Lucy was vigorously stirring eggs on the burner next to his. He said, breaking a silence that was becoming intolerable, "You'll wear out the bottom of the saucepan."

She dropped the spoon. "Troy, please don't go."

"I'm not going anywhere until after breakfast."

"I don't mean——"

"Hi," said Stephen. "Where's my mum?"

Lucy gaped at him. Troy said, "Your mum had a baby in the night... Do you want to go and see them both?"

Stephen stood rooted to the spot. "It wasn't supposed to come for two more weeks. What kind of baby?"

"A girl," Troy supplied, noticing that the intrepid Stephen looked scared out of his wits. "Shall I go with you?"

Stephen nodded, his sleep-tousled hair flopping over his forehead. "Does it cry a lot?"

"Not so far," Troy said cheerfully. "But she'll cry sometimes."

He led the way into Anna's bedroom. Anna opened her eyes and smiled at her son. "Come and see your new sister, Stephen."

Stephen was warily tiptoeing round the end of the bed as Troy left the room and returned to the kitchen. Lucy was still stirring the eggs; he started to turn the bacon. As if he hadn't left, Lucy said over-loudly, "I meant I don't want you to leave the island. That's what I meant."

Hot fat spattered the back of Troy's hand. Swearing under his breath, he turned down the gas. "I'm going, Lucy."

"Please don't go," she cried. "I know I haven't——"

Fiercely he interrupted her. "I'm leaving because I can't be around you and not be able to make love with you. That's——"

"Breakfast nearly ready?" asked the birder who had led the charge upstairs in the middle of the night.

Lucy closed her eyes. "It'll be ready in five minutes," she said in a strangled voice.

"We'll want our lunches too," he said helpfully.

Lucy favored him with a false, brilliant smile. "You shall have them—I promise."

He retreated to the dining-room. "Men!" Lucy exploded, and shoved the pot of eggs to the back of the stove. "I know that's what it comes down to, Troy. But——"

The side door opened and Mrs Mossop steamed in with Hubert in her wake. "What's this about a baby?" Hubert said, flourishing an untidy bouquet of purple asters and goldenrod.

"I knew it would be a girl," Mrs Mossop crowed. "She was carrying it high and it's a full moon besides."

"How did you find out so fast?" Lucy demanded.

"Keith phoned me and I phoned Mrs Mossop," Hubert said. "Keith's in seventh heaven."

He must be, Troy thought, to make a phone call voluntarily. "Stephen's in with Anna at the moment," he said. "How about a cup of coffee?"

Mrs Mossop bent a dark look on Troy. "Everything's all right, is it? She had a craving for mushrooms in the third month, and that had me worried."

"A healthy and beautiful baby," Troy said firmly.

"Breakfast's ready," Lucy interjected, pushing her hair back from her face. "I'm going to serve the crew in the dining-room, Troy. Could you cut bread for sandwiches for me?"

Mrs Mossop ignored the bustle in the kitchen and said magistrally, "Come along, Hubert, let's go and see the baby."

In a procession of two they paraded past the stove and out into the hall. Troy said, trying not to laugh, "In exactly ten minutes I'm going to exercise my authority as Anna's personal physician and turf everyone out of her room except the baby. In the meantime, I'll cut some bread."

"Thank you," Lucy said, and departed for the dining-room.

Troy was buttering the bread by the time she came back. She opened a big can of tuna and said, "Clarence does his regular run in three days—couldn't you wait until then?"

"Why, Lucy?" Troy answered bluntly. "What's the point in prolonging the agony? I've already said I can forgo having a family for the sake of being with you. But I can't live with you and not be able to make love with you—for Pete's sake, I surely don't have to explain how impossible that is?"

"Sorry to interrupt," Quentin said breezily, poking his head round the kitchen door. "What's this about a new baby?"

Lucy picked up the bread knife and brandished it in the air. "If one more person walks into this kitchen," she stormed, "I won't be responsible for the consequences!"

"Troy's right, you know," Quentin said, his blue eyes sparkling. "No man worthy of the name could live with you without wanting to take you to bed, Lucy, my love. You've really got to get over this hang-up you have about sex."

"Go and see the baby, Quentin," Lucy ordered, scowling. "And stay out of my kitchen for the rest of the day."

"Keith phoned me," Quentin added unnecessarily. "Couldn't believe it—he talked my ear off. I reckon he'll tell Clarence this baby is more important than hauling a few lobster traps. They could be here any minute."

Lucy looked hunted, and Troy's smile faded. Quentin gave a broad grin, raised his hand in salute and disappeared from the doorway. Lucy said fractiously, "I've never noticed what an aggressive smile he has. Full of teeth."

Quentin had admirable teeth. Troy asked, "What are you giving the birders to drink with their lunch?"

"Arsenic. Bleach. I don't care!"

Lucy had always looked magnificent in a rage—her very hair sparking with energy, her eyes like storm-clouds. Troy said, "I'm going back with Clarence, Lucy."

Her breath hissed between her teeth. She aligned the bread knife with the edge of the bread board as if her whole life depended on getting them exactly parallel.

"I've never begged you for anything before, Troy. I always said that if I had to beg, there was no point. But I'm begging you now—please don't go today. The birth of the baby, it did something to——"

Keith burst into the kitchen from the dining-room door, his red hair windblown, his shirt done up on all the wrong buttons. Seizing Troy by the arm, he said, "Is Anna okay? And the baby?"

"They're both fine," Troy said. "In fact, I'll go in there right now and get rid of all the visitors so you can get near her and see for yourself. Give me two minutes."

He went to Anna's door, and with an impartial smile said, "Stephen, your dad's in the kitchen. I'm going to ask everyone else to leave while I make sure that Anna's doing all right."

What Lucy called his "hospital voice" worked fine here. Once the room was empty, Anna said, "Thanks—it's lovely of everyone to come, but I'm tired out. Is Keith really here, Troy?"

Quickly he checked her over. "I'll send him in. No more visitors except him and Stephen for a while, Anna. You need your rest."

He called them from the apartment door. Stephen and Keith went in together, the little boy clutching his father's hand. Troy shut the bedroom door softly behind them. Then he leaned against the wall, aware in every bone in his body that he had been up all night and that his brain seemed to be stuck in low gear. What in hell was he going to do about Lucy?

He should go straight to the wharf and tell Clarence he was going back with him.

He had to say goodbye to Lucy first. He'd be the worst kind of coward otherwise. Pushing himself upright, Troy went back to the kitchen.

Clarence wasn't at the wharf; he was standing by the stove drinking coffee. Quentin was leaning against the counter, his pencil flying over the page of a small sketchbook. Hubert and Mrs Mossop were sitting at the kitchen table with a pot of tea, the asters and goldenrod teetering in a vase that was much too small for them. Lucy was wrapping sandwiches in waxed paper. She looked tired and harassed and—strangely enough, in a roomful of people—lonely.

It scarcely seemed the setting for putting an end to his marriage. Even less so when the birders crowded in to pick up their lunches. Lucy, to her credit, was entirely civil to them. Absently Troy helped himself to a rasher of bacon.

Across the room Lucy's eyes met his. She still looked tired, harassed and lonely; she also looked desperate. She closed the refrigerator door, threaded her way past Clarence, who was laughing at something Hubert had said and looked in no hurry to get back to his lobster pots, and came to stand in front of Troy. No one was paying them the slightest bit of attention.

She said incoherently, "When I held the baby, it was so light, so tiny, so perfectly formed . . . I was able to do that, Troy. I was able to help Anna and to hold her baby. Yesterday I would have said I couldn't possibly have done either one of those things. When you asked me to help I said I couldn't, and I thought I was telling the truth. But I wasn't."

She fell silent; unconsciously she was pulling at a thread on her apron. Troy wanted to take her into his arms and hold her, and fought the impulse with all his might. "What are you getting at?" he asked evenly.

"We did make love, even though I said I'd never do that again. It was heaven to be with you. I felt like I'd come back to myself. Back home. It was only after-wards..." Staring fixedly at his shirtfront she said, "The last twelve hours have turned everything upside-down—I don't know where I am or what I believe. Things that I thought would never change have changed. I—I don't trust myself any more."

She was being as honest as she knew how; Troy would have sworn to that. Swept by a wave of love for her so strong that he felt it judder through his body, and forcing his hands to stay at his sides, he said, "Lucy, I love you. I want to be with you. But if every time we make love you're going to be terrified of getting pregnant—I don't think I can handle that."

"Stay until Friday," she pleaded. "Don't go back today."

Clarence plunked his empty mug on the counter and drawled, "Well, I better get goin'. Told the wife I'd take her to town this afternoon—doesn't do to keep her waitin'. Any messages or errands anyone wants done?"

Lucy's eyes flew upwards to Troy's face. He looked over at Clarence, his jaw clamped. It would only take a minute to throw his stuff together; common sense dic-tated that he leave now, that he had done more than enough to try and revive his marriage and that anything more bordered on masochism. But common sense had never had much to do with the way he felt about Lucy. He said, in a voice that sounded almost normal, "Nothing for me, thanks, Clarence."

Lucy's whole body sagged with relief. "I was so afraid you'd go," she whispered.

And Troy, who might have expected to feel elation at a decision made, or at least relief that he now knew what he was doing for the next three days, felt only a huge fatigue settle on him.

Hubert got up from the table and called out, "Maybe tonight you could check on the petrels, Lucy, as it's a full moon—take Troy with you. The birders want to sleep all night because they're going out with Clarence first thing tomorrow to find shearwaters."

Lucy nodded mechanically. Hubert and Clarence then said their goodbyes, Clarence clutching two letters Hubert had given him. Mrs Mossop began rinsing plates in the sink. And Quentin sauntered over to Troy and Lucy.

He tore a page from his book and held it out to Lucy. "What do you think? Will she like it?"

Lucy took it. It was a simple pencil sketch of Anna with the baby in her arms. Lucy stammered, "It's b-beautiful. Excuse me, I've got to go to the bathroom," and ran from the kitchen, still clutching the sketch.

"I hope she doesn't cry all over it," Quentin said. "I did another sketch. For you, Troy." And he tore out a second sheet.

Troy looked down at the sheet of paper. He and Lucy were facing each other, not touching. All their unhappiness and struggle had been delineated in a few sure strokes of Quentin's pencil; the love that bound them together as adversaries was so obvious that his throat closed with pain.

"I was going to leave this morning," he said.

"'Never give advice'—that's what my old man used to tell me," Quentin remarked. "But my theory is that rules are made to be broken. So I think you should go out to the petrels with Lucy tonight. I'm not sure what it is, but there's something about those birds that touches her." He clapped Troy on the shoulder. "In the meantime, by the look of you, you should catch up on some sleep."

"Now, that is good advice," Troy rejoined, dredging up a smile.

Quentin signed one corner of the sketch. He said gruffly, "I watched Lucy all summer. She was like a bird blown way off course that's landed in a strange place where it doesn't feel at home. But it's lost its bearings and can't find the way to its real destination." He grimaced in self-derision. "Hell, I should've been a poet, not an artist. You can have this if you like."

Troy took the piece of paper and said awkwardly, "Thanks, Quentin."

"No sweat. I'd better get back to work. Good luck."

When Troy went out into the hall, Lucy was still locked in the bathroom. He went upstairs, stripped off his clothes and fell into bed. He was asleep before Clarence's boat left for the mainland.

CHAPTER NINE

TROY slept most of the day, waking a couple of hours before dinner. He showered, then went downstairs and checked on Anna. The baby, who was to be called Jennifer, was sleeping soundly, and Anna herself had had a bath and had sat in the sun on the deck for an hour.

"I'm feeling much better," she said. "I'm so glad Keith is home; he really wanted a little girl. And I'm glad you're staying, Troy. You and Lucy belong together." She hesitated. "The only trouble is, I don't know what to make of Stephen. I don't think he's jealous—that's not it. He just seems at a loss. Not the slightest bit enthusiastic about the baby. Maybe if you see him, you could talk to him?"

"I'll try," Troy promised. But before he went in search of Stephen he went to the kitchen, where Lucy was rolling out pastry for chicken pot pies. She gave him a wary smile. "Did you get any rest today?" he asked.

"I slept from ten until three. So I should be able to go out to the petrels for a while tonight."

"Can I come with you?"

She swallowed. "Yes," she said.

Something tight-held in Troy relaxed a little. He said, "You've got flour on your cheek," and reached out to brush it away. Her skin was warm and soft and smooth. He put his hands in his pockets.

Lucy said impetuously, "I never stopped wanting you, Troy. Never."

157

"I know that now," he said. "But it's too bad you couldn't have told me a year ago."

"How could I? I had to keep you at a distance because I knew I'd never risk having any more children. If you believed I didn't want you any more—well, that just made it easier. Or not quite so difficult."

Troy spoke the exact truth. "I didn't understand how you could turn desire off, like a kitchen tap. One day you wanted me, the next day you didn't. I didn't know how you could turn *me* off, basically. I felt—repudiated. The upshot was that I began to doubt all the times we'd been together and been so happy. Maybe you'd been acting. Maybe you really hadn't wanted me nearly as much as I thought you had. Or maybe I bored you."

She looked aghast. "Oh, Troy...if you only knew how many times over the last year I've woken in the night reaching for you."

"Let's promise each other something, Lucy. No matter what happens over the next three days there'll be no more deception between us."

"The truth, the whole truth, and nothing but the truth?" she said with a weak smile.

"It's the only way we'll rebuild trust," Troy said forcibly. Although what was the good of rebuilding trust if she was still afraid to take him as her lover?

"All right," she said. "I promise."

"So do I." He looked at the clock. "Why don't we meet around eleven tonight?"

"Sounds good. That way I can have a bit of a rest after dinner."

He only had until Friday. Troy leaned over the counter and kissed Lucy with all the love and passion that was in him. Her response was all he could have wished; her hands buried in his hair, she pulled him closer and kissed him back, until his head was swimming and his back hurt from bending across the countertop.

When they were eventually disentangled from each other, Lucy said breathlessly, "There's flour in your hair; it makes you look very distinguished. I think as you grow older you'll just get handsomer and handsomer." Then she looked down at the pie crust as though she wasn't sure what it was. Picking up the rolling pin and wielding it as though it were a baseball bat, she flattened a mound of pastry. "I love you, Troy... Oh, Troy, I do love you—I never stopped. How could I?"

"You're ruining that piece of pastry," Troy said.

She gave a weak giggle. "I'll feed it to the birders; they're always so busy comparing notes I'm not sure they notice what they eat." Then she looked up, and there was a sudden sheen of tears in her eyes. "Before I came to work this afternoon, I went to see Anna and the baby."

Troy said quietly, "I'm proud of you, Lucy."

"I'm trying very hard to stop running away," she gulped. "From—from Michael, I mean."

"I shouldn't have called you a coward."

"Yes, you should. *I* shouldn't have left you and gone to Ottawa. I just didn't know what else to *do*."

"You think I didn't make any mistakes?" Troy said violently. "This morning I accused you of never comforting me—the truth is I only rarely gave you the opportunity. I was too busy keeping my feelings under wraps. My rationale was that it wouldn't help you if I let them all hang out. That I was protecting you." His smile was lop-sided. "The reality was that I was into macho, stiff-upper-lip stuff."

"Oh...the same thing you did with your sister?"

"That's right. An old pattern reasserting itself."

He could see her thinking back. "You did seem incredibly strong, as though you had everything under control—I remember that now. It made me feel even worse, because I was always on the verge of falling to pieces."

"I waited to fall apart until after you'd gone. So maybe your leaving wasn't such a bad thing after all."

Her eyes filled with tears. "Just to hear you say that makes me feel so much better."

"I should have said it long before this."

"Hindsight's always easy, Troy."

He went on steadily, "If I hadn't suggested we have a second child, maybe you wouldn't have left."

A tear dripped on to her hand. "If you only knew how horribly guilty I've felt about... Oh, God, is that Mrs Mossop? Will we ever have a conversation that's not interrupted by sixteen other people? And if I weep all over the pastry even the birders won't eat it."

Mrs Mossop's stately tread was approaching from the dining-room. Troy said, "Dearest, darling and adorable Lucy, I love you. I'll see you tonight at eleven." He kissed the tip of her nose and hurried out into the hall. *He* was a coward, he thought with an inner spurt of laughter. There were times he could deal with Mrs Mossop and times when it was expedient to remove himself from her vicinity as speedily as an Olympic sprinter.

But even though she'd interrupted them, he had said something he'd badly needed to say. From the best of motives he'd tried to protect Lucy from his feelings; quite probably it had been the worst thing he could have done. If he'd given Lucy a choice, she wouldn't have opted for protection. She'd have wanted him to be real.

Forgiveness, Troy thought slowly. That's what this is all about.

He went outside. Chickadees were chattering in the branches of the maple trees. Reminded that he was supposed to talk to Stephen, he looked around.

The boy was nowhere to be seen in the vicinity of the inn. Following his instincts, Troy took the path to the western shore, and it was on the rocks that looked out to Fishhead Island that he found Stephen, sitting hunched over, staring at the ocean.

Gusts of wind ruffled the surface of the water to darkness, like clouds chasing each other across the sea. Whitecaps burst against the shores of the island in showers of spray. Troy walked closer, his steps rattling among the stones. "Stephen? You okay?"

"Yeah," said Stephen, pounding two rocks together and avoiding Troy's eyes.

"Your mother's worried about you."

"Everyone keeps saying how beautiful the baby is," Stephen burst out. "I don't think she's beautiful. I think she's ugly. Her face is all squished together."

Troy sat down so he was on a level with Stephen. He said, "That's because she's so new. Being born is very hard work for a baby, and you're right, she does look squished—that's what happens when she's actually born. But in a day or two that'll wear off and she'll look just the way you pictured her."

"Really?" Stephen asked.

"Really."

"Oh. Mum had this magazine she showed me, and it had photos of babies and they were all kind of cute. Not like Jennifer." He added in a small voice, "I thought there was something wrong with her and no one was telling me."

His heart full of compassion, Troy said, "Stephen, I'm a doctor, and I swear to you there's not one thing wrong with Jennifer. I'd tell you if there were."

There were tears hanging on Stephen's lashes. "Mrs Mossop said my mum ate some mushrooms, and so when I saw the baby I thought the mushrooms must have done it." He bulged out his cheeks. "She sort of looked like a mushroom."

The boy's logic was impeccable. Cursing Mrs Mossop and her dire predictions, Troy said, "You don't have to believe everything you hear, Stephen. Especially from Mrs Mossop—she's a very fine woman who talks too much. I promise you that Jennifer will be every bit as cute as those babies you saw in the magazine."

"I couldn't ask Mum or Dad, you see," Stephen snuffled.

Troy put his arm around the boy and held on hard, and at the appropriate moment produced a clean handkerchief from his jacket pocket. "Want to go back now?" he asked.

Stephen scrambled to his feet. "I gotta think of a present for the baby," he said.

"Maybe you could color her a picture?"

"I s'pose I could draw an owl." Stephen's face brightened. "Or I could give her a seashell." He glanced over at the island, where the seals were moaning. "A really special one."

"You could go through all your collections."

Stephen skipped up the bank. "Is it nearly dinner-time? I'm hungry."

Stephen, so Troy discovered on the walk home, hadn't eaten breakfast or lunch. "Why don't you go into the kitchen?" Troy said when they arrived back at the inn. "I bet Lucy would find you a cookie or an apple. And do you mind if I tell your dad what was the matter, Stephen?"

"Nope." Throwing Troy a smile over his shoulder, Stephen went inside.

Troy wandered over to the woodshed, where Keith was splitting kindling, and relayed the gist of Stephen's fears. Keith listened with his whole attention, then nodded. "Makes sense. I'll tell Anna. Thanks."

Keith's words might be few but his smile through the forest of his beard was warm. Troy went to dinner well pleased that he had stayed on the island. The chicken pot pie was delicious, and as he helped himself to another slice he was thinking with anticipation that at eleven o'clock he would have Lucy to himself.

Even if they did have to head into the woods to achieve any degree of privacy.

Troy dressed warmly for the expedition to the petrels, because the wind was still strong and there was a chill in the air that presaged the end of summer. As he pulled on a jacket over his forest-green sweater and navy cords he was humming tunelessly to himself. He was going to see Lucy. A Lucy who had begged him to stay on the island. A Lucy who was changing in front of his eyes. He laced up his hiking boots, took his flashlight and left the inn.

Lucy was wearing a wool sweater as well, hers a patchwork of autumn colors that shifted and blended like the leaves on the trees. She looked very beautiful. "Neat sweater," Troy said.

"Marcia knitted it."

"It doesn't look like Marcia."

"No, it doesn't, does it? She read a book by some man who designs sweaters and decided she should try. I'm wearing her first and only effort."

Such passionate and spontaneous colors didn't belong to Troy's image of his elder sister-in-law. "Maybe she's in love?" he said.

"Marcia? Not likely," Lucy snorted. "There, I'm ready. All we have to do is walk the trails and check on predators—there won't be much going on with a full moon."

Once they were out of range of the lights of the inn, the moon was bright enough that they didn't need flashlights; stars poked pinholes of light through the black velvet canopy of the sky. Lucy led the way along the trail, which was edged by shrubs whose leaves rustled in the wind. The whickering of the petrel chicks soon cut through all the other sounds—primitive cries of hunger that were sharp and imperative.

As though this had reminded her, Lucy said, "I'm glad you found out what was bothering Stephen. I couldn't understand why he didn't want anything to do with the baby. I put it down to jealousy, I guess." Perhaps given courage by the darkness, she added impulsively, "You were always such a good father, Troy."

"Turn around, Lucy, I want to see your face." As she obeyed him he said, "I can't imagine anyone being a more loving and attentive mother than you were."

The moonlight cast shadows on her face. She whispered, "We didn't get much time to be his parents, though, did we?"

"No. But we gave it all we had in the time we did have."

"No guarantees—that's what you're saying."

"None whatsoever," Troy said.

Her features were unreadable. "We'd better get on—Hubert wanted me to go as far as the shore, because that's where the gulls hang out."

Troy said implacably, "You're still running away, Lucy—and we've only got until Friday."

"It's too cold to stand around talking," Lucy said irritably, and took off through the trees.

He'd come out here with the express purpose of forcing another confrontation, Troy realized as he followed her along the path. What use was forgiveness if she was too scared to make love to him?

The occasional petrel shot through the air over Troy's head while the chorus of cries rose and fell around his feet. He didn't want another mate and another burrow; he knew that in his bones. He wanted the woman he'd married and the home in Vancouver that was still full of her presence.

The home that had an empty nursery.

Troy lengthened his stride. He'd told Lucy he could manage without more children, and he'd meant it. But he was no saint. Would he eventually resent her for depriving him of the small miracle that had taken place in Anna's room last night?

When the path widened into a clearing at the edge of the ocean, Troy came up behind Lucy. The tall trees that grew inland had tapered to wind-pruned, hunched shapes. The white-fringed rocks, the white light glittering coldly on the water, the white shapes of gulls waiting for the petrels to come in to land—all seemed ominous and inimical to Troy. He shivered involuntarily, wishing he was in his bed and Lucy in his arms.

In a blur of movement a black shape detached itself from a tree and launched itself at a petrel in mid-flight.

The bird's death cry lacerated Troy's ears; like an echo he heard Lucy cry out in horror.

The owl—for he was sure it had been an owl—had vanished with its prey. Swiftly Troy closed the distance between himself and Lucy and wrapped his arms around her, pulling her back to his chest, feeling the softness of her breasts under his wrists.

She said numbly, "Its mate won't ever know what happened to it. And their chick might die..."

Then she suddenly twisted in his arms, burrowing her face into his sweater in a wild storm of tears that erupted from nowhere and whose violence appalled Troy. Sobs tore their way from her throat and her body was shuddering, her fingers digging into his spine as though he was her only lifeline. Troy held her close, his cheek pressing on her hair, striving through his very stillness and strength to give her the comfort of his presence.

And then, as though the talons of the owl had ripped his own flesh, he heard the one word that she was whimpering over and over again. Their son's name. Michael.

It had taken an island thousands of miles from home and many long months for Lucy to turn to him for solace. Grief and gratitude swirling through his body like the changing of the tides, Troy kissed her hair, murmuring small, meaningless phrases of consolation until gradually she quietened in his arms. He tugged the folds of his jacket around her to keep her warm and said, "That's been cooped up for a long time."

"Mmm." Her breath was coming in little hiccups. She scrabbled in her pocket and blew her nose, still standing in the circle of his arms. In a low voice she said, "The petrel dying like that...life can be horribly cruel, and we're so vulnerable when we love someone."

"I'm not sure that anything comes without a cost."

"No safety, though—ever?"

Troy said with passionate conviction, "We can only love, Lucy... That's all we can do. And sometimes, for each one of us, and often at huge cost, love and loss intertwine. But anything else isn't living at all."

"You see that every day at the hospital."

"True enough. Although when it hit home with my own child, I realized I knew virtually nothing."

Feather-light, Lucy kissed his cheek, her words tumbling one over the other. "I'm so sorry I closed myself off from you. There was this weight of inertia pressing down on me, this deep hole I'd fallen into... I couldn't look after myself, let alone you."

"Neither one of us was able to help the other, Lucy. But even through the worst of it, you never stopped loving me."

"I never did, no." She bit her lip. "But I panicked every time you came near me, because I was sure if we made love I'd shatter into a thousand fragments and never come back together again." Her smile was twisted. "Like Humpty Dumpty. And then, later on, we did make love a couple of times and it was awful—do you remember that?"

Troy did, only too well. "It was so obvious you were forcing yourself to be with me—that was what I hated. Something that had always been so natural and spontaneous had become an obligation. It made me lonelier than I'd ever been in my life."

"Separate solitudes," Lucy said with a shiver. "When my body retreated from you my soul sort of withered away, so that I couldn't stand being with you. I really did think you'd be better off without me."

Playing with the neckline of his sweater, she went on, "I'd always prided myself on being the only member of

the Barnes family who was in touch with her feelings.
But by the time I went back to Ottawa I felt as if my
whole self-image was false. I'd been put to the test and
I couldn't handle my emotions. I'd had to run away from
them. It was the rest of my family who had all the
emotions. Catherine ranted and raved at me for leaving
you, Marcia treated me as though I was on the verge of
collapse, and Mother—well, Mother was less than happy
with me and made no secret of it.''

She was now rubbing her palms rhythmically up and
down his chest. ''After I saw you last spring I came here
and took off my wedding-ring and used my maiden name
and tried to learn how to live without you. I was sure
you'd want a divorce sooner or later, so I suppose I was
trying to prepare myself for that.'' She gave him a watery
grin. ''I hated it when you asked for one, though.''

Troy cut to the heart of the matter. ''Are you coming
back to Vancouver with me, Lucy?''

''You're sure you want me to?''

''Yes.''

The very brevity of his reply seemed to give her
courage. ''I want to—oh, God, how I want to! For
months I've felt like a boat that's been cut adrift from
its moorings...but underneath it all I'm still afraid,
Troy.''

With all the force of his personality, Troy said, ''We
can never know when the owl will strike. But to bury
ourselves under the ground so as to escape danger isn't
any kind of an answer.''

''When I held Jennifer today I...I scarcely knew what
I felt. She's so beautiful—so soft and warm and trusting.
Because, of course, that's another thing that went wrong.
I've always believed touch is so important—that's why
I give massages—and I always loved touching Michael.

His skin was so delicate, almost transparent. When he was gone I felt betrayed at such a deep level. Something I'd trusted in totally had been snatched away. After that, I couldn't bring myself to touch anyone—all the way from my clients to you, my own husband. When I massaged Anna's back last night, it was the first time in a year and a half I've done anything like that." She gave him a troubled smile. "It felt fine."

Stubbornly Troy repeated his question. "So are you going to move back in with me?"

She said in a rush, "Maybe some day I'll be ready to have another child, Troy—but I don't know that I have the right to ask you to wait."

"If you can't welcome me to your bed, we're finished. That's the issue for me." With what might have seemed like cruelty Troy added, "The odds of our second child dying of crib death are so small as to be infinitesimal."

The shock of his words ran through her frame. "My head tells me you're right. But fear's got nothing to do with reason."

He said urgently, "Before all this happened our love-making had so many different moods—it could be comfortable and companionable, or dreamlike, or full of good old-fashioned lust. But sometimes, for both of us, the earth would shift. It was the lifeblood of our marriage, Lucy, the outward sign of all that was between us. I can't live with you and be afraid to touch you."

Her voice was full of torment, like the death-note of the petrel. "How do I stop being afraid?"

He had promised to tell the truth. "I don't know," Troy said.

Lucy sagged against him. "I'm so tired... can we go back?"

"Yeah," he said, releasing her, "we'd better go back."

He followed her down the trail, his guts churning. He'd wanted a confrontation, hadn't he? Well, he'd gotten it. But if he'd hoped for simple answers, he'd been disappointed.

Twenty minutes later they arrived at Lucy's cabin. She turned to face him on the porch. "Goodnight, Troy. I'm so glad we talked."

The walk had given Troy time to think. Ruthlessly he cut across her softly spoken words. "Lucy, I want to sleep with you."

She took a step backward. "No—we can't! I'm not protected against a pregnancy."

That that should be her first response still had the power to wound. Troy said flatly, "I said sleep, not make love. Tonight's not the time to start anything we can't finish—we were both up all last night and you've just cried your eyes out. All I want to do is sleep in your bed, Lucy. Sleep, literally."

"You don't know when to quit, do you?"

"We've got to start somewhere," he said, in a tone as inflexible as steel.

Her lashes fell. "All right," she said ungraciously, and unlatched the door.

The cabin felt cold. Using his flashlight, Troy went over to the woodstove and bundled in some paper and kindling. He struck a match, watching the paper flare up, then crinkle into blackness as the flames devoured it. As the wood took hold he added a couple of small logs, angling them upward. By the time he closed the glass door flames were leaping up the flue, throwing flickering shadows on the ceiling.

As he stood up Lucy came out of the bathroom. She was wearing a cotton nightgown that swathed her from head to foot; the firelight glimmered in her hair. "Do you know what's so ridiculous about this?" she announced. "I know you better than anyone else in the world, and I feel as though I've invited a total stranger into my bed. Figure that one out, will you?"

"If it's any help, I feel much the same way."

She clambered into bed and pulled the covers up to her chin. "I've got to be up at six," she said in a staccato voice. "The birders want breakfast before they go out with Clarence. I think Keith's going, too."

"Then you'd better set the alarm," Troy said, and went into the bathroom.

When he came out, he'd stripped to his underwear. He laid his neatly folded clothes on the table and walked over to the bed. Lucy's eyes were huge, and he was almost certain she was regretting having agreed to this. Making no attempt to kiss her, or even touch her, he climbed into bed and turned his back on her. "Goodnight," he said, and closed his eyes.

"Goodnight," she mumbled.

He lay very still, listening to the wind sigh in the trees and the nearer, homely crackling of the flames. Through them both he could hear Lucy breathing—short, shallow breaths, eloquent of tension. After waiting a few minutes, he said, "You could cuddle up to my back, if you wanted to."

In a small voice she said, "I always used to cuddle up to your chest to fall asleep."

"If you were to do that now, you'd know I was giving you a double message. Head saying sleep. Body saying sleep later, thank you very much. Seems to me we promised not to give each other any double messages."

Lucy's tiny snort of laughter encouraged Troy immensely. She said decorously, "So we did."

He heard the bed creak as she wriggled closer. Then he felt the soft swell of her breasts against his spine and the small weight of her palm on his ribs. He exclaimed, "You're cold."

"I got cold out in the woods."

Still keeping his back to her, he drew her closer, curling his body so she could fit into it; with tiny snuggling motions that shivered through him she rested her cheek to his shoulderblade and gave a long sigh. "That feels better," she said.

Her hands gradually warmed against his flesh. Her breathing slowed. Aware of her presence in every cell of his body, Troy slid one hand to lie on her hip. Then, again, he closed his eyes.

When next he opened them, the little clock beside the bed said five to six; he had long ago trained himself to wake before the alarm. He had turned over in the night and Lucy now lay curled into his chest, an old habit reasserting itself. Her hair smelled sweetly of the floral shampoo she used; his arms encircled her hips. Lightheaded with love and desire, Troy wished he could stay where he was for the rest of the day.

In a series of piercing beeps the alarm clock announced that it was six o'clock. Lucy's eyes flew open and her arm swept round to shut it off. In the sudden silence she gasped, "I wasn't dreaming, then!"

"Dreaming what, my darling?" Troy said lazily.

Her cheeks flamed scarlet. "Never you mind."

"Are you suggesting I use my imagination?"

"It would need to be very explicit."

"On the basis of past experience, I'm sure I could make it so. Good morning, Lucy."

"There's nothing remotely funny about this," she said truculently. "So why am I laughing? Troy, I've got to go to work."

"You won't have to go to work at eight o'clock this evening."

"You're pushing me too hard!"

"The boat leaves on Friday. And you're the one who asked me to stay."

She rolled away from him, and with a thud her bare feet hit the floor. "Mrs Mossop's doing dinner today and the birders won't be back for lunch. So why don't we go for a walk after breakfast?"

Troy didn't want to go for a walk. He wanted to go to bed with his wife. "If that's your best offer," he said coolly.

"I should personally have escorted you to Clarence's boat yesterday," she fumed, stalked to the bathroom and shut the door with the nearest thing to a slam that the flimsy wooden panels would allow.

Troy put his hands behind his head and gazed up at the ceiling. It would be very romantic to imagine that while they were on their walk they might make love on a patch of soft moss under the dancing shadows of the trees; he still had a yen to do that. But there was no drugstore on the island and it would be criminal of him to expose Lucy to the risk of pregnancy twice in a row. Even if she'd agree to make love. Which he doubted.

Physically frustrated, and mentally out of sorts, Troy turned on to his stomach and began an alphabetical listing of the nerves and blood vessels that supplied the face. It was an exercise that since his days as an intern had been guaranteed to put him to sleep.

Except that this morning it didn't work.

CHAPTER TEN

AT A little past eleven Troy and Lucy emerged from the woods that bordered the western shore; other than commonplaces, they'd spoken little on the walk. Although the wind was brisk enough to toss spume from the crests of the waves, the sun was shining brightly. The brier roses were fully open, their delicate scent sweetening the salt tang of the sea.

Gazing out at the ocean, Lucy said abruptly, "You know, I was meant to come to this island, Troy. Anna's pregnancy, my friendship with Stephen, Quentin's painting, the petrels . . . I've changed over the summer; I know I have."

It was a plea for understanding, and she looked very beautiful standing knee-deep in the gold discs of the sow thistles. "But has anything really changed?" Troy said heavily. "You're still afraid to make love."

"I'm committed to stay here until Anna and Keith close up, in three weeks. But then I could come back to Vancouver," she said obliquely.

"To separate bedrooms?" Troy asked, suddenly angry.

"Dammit, I don't know!" She scowled at him. "Let's go and listen to the seals on Fishhead Island."

The island was surrounded by foam, like a collar bordered with white lace on a garment of deepest blue. The seals were silent. But as Troy casually glanced along the ridge of rocks, from one end to the other, he stiffened. Raising his binoculars, he focused on the patch of color that had caught his attention near the north end of the island—a color unlike that of either a seal or a bird.

In the round field of his binoculars he saw a rowboat with a small boy at the oars. Stephen, wearing a bright orange life-jacket. The boat was caught among the rocks, bucking on the waves like a wild horse; to his horror he saw water splash over the bow as the stern bashed into a rock. Stephen shoved at the rock with one oar.

Troy dropped the binoculars on the stones. "Stephen's out there. Help me get the other boat into the water." As he surged to his feet he saw what he had moments ago ignored: the long gouge in the shale where Stephen had dragged the lighter of the two boats to the water's edge.

Lucy, admirably, said not one word. They raced to the treeline, overturned the other rowboat and, one on each side, lugged it down to the water. Then Troy ran back for the oars while Lucy jammed the oarlocks into their slots. As she steadied the boat, knee-deep in the water, Troy sat on the center thwart and placed the oars. From the corner of his eye he saw Lucy about to climb aboard.

Over his shoulder he yelled, "Go and get Quentin, Lucy. See if he has a lifebuoy. Or at the very least some rope."

"I'm going with you!"

"You can't—I'll need help getting into shore. *Go* Lucy!"

In the split-second as she hesitated he could see her fight against his logic and then accept it—a small, fierce battle that told him more than words. "I hate leaving you," she cried. "I'll be as fast as I can."

He was already angling the oars. "Push off so I'm headed into the waves, will you? And then hurry."

Over the metallic slap of the swell against the aluminum prow he heard her shout, "Troy, I love you—be careful, won't you?" Then the currents seized him and he began to row, bending from his hips to get maximum leverage.

The wind was offshore, gusting in Troy's face. His shirt was soon soaked with spray, his jeans plastered to his thighs. Bracing his feet, he put every ounce of his muscle power into each stroke, glancing over his shoulder to keep on track. As the waves lifted him he caught sight of Stephen's boat sliding into a trough. In sheer panic he realized the boy had lost one of his oars. He dug his own into the water and pulled harder than he'd ever pulled in his life.

He hadn't been able to save Michael's life. He had to save Stephen's.

The wind, at least, was in his favor. Grimly Troy leaned forward and pulled back, leaned and pulled, again and again, water slurping round his feet, spray stinging his cheeks. He was panting for breath when he next checked behind him; but he was only a few feet from Stephen's boat. Making a lightning-swift calculation of wind and waves, he dug his right oar in and swung the boat round. "Push off the rocks with your oar, Stephen," he shouted. "Over this way."

He managed to ship one oar before the two boats collided with an ugly screech. He reached out for the boy, clasping him by the shoulder, bodily hauling him aboard seconds before an expanse of foam yawned between the rowboats. "Keep down low—grab hold of my ankles."

There was no time even to think of towing Stephen's boat, because of the danger of being pinned to the rocks by the wind. Troy didn't dare try to land either; the breakers were smashing against the shore, flinging curtains of sunlit spray high in the air. He struggled to bring the boat round again, grunting with effort as he fought the vicious force of the sea.

A wave broke broadside over the gunwale, flattening Stephen to Troy's knee. The boy reached for the bailer and began tossing water over the side. Adrenaline racing through his veins, Troy yanked on the oars with the strength of two men until, to his infinite relief, the prow headed toward the land.

They'd shipped enough water that the boat felt sluggish, and he was rowing against the wind. But Stephen was crouched at his feet and with every dig of the oars the rocks of Fishhead Island were receding. His back was now bearing the brunt of the spray; he was glad Stephen was sheltered by his body.

They had crossed the stretch of open water and were fast approaching the rocks that rose like huge walruses among the chaos of waves. Troy altered course, feeling every muscle from his shoulders to his wrists crying out for rest. "We'll try and land in that open spot," he yelled. "Don't get out of the boat until I tell you."

He dipped the oars and pulled with all his might. But his left oar struck a boulder beneath the water; the shock jarred its way up his arm. The boat lurched crazily. Gritting his teeth, Troy strove to straighten it. Stephen piped, "Lucy and Quentin are on the beach."

They must have run the whole way. "The boat feels like a tank," he panted. "Keep bailing, Stephen."

Stephen was peering round Troy's knees. "Quentin's in the water—he's got a rope."

"If he throws it, do your best to catch it," Troy ordered, and risked a glance at the shore.

With a horrible grinding of metal on granite the boat crashed into a rock that had been hidden by the spray.

Stephen was thrown sideways. Troy grabbed for him, saw the water rushing up to meet him, and held on to the boy with the last of his strength as the waves closed over his head. His feet sought the bottom and found only water; he stroked upward and heaved Stephen above the surface, filling his own lungs with air.

Something slashed at the side of his face, burning like fire. Quentin's rope, he realized crazily, and seized it before the current could steal it from him. Treading water, he said as forcefully as he could, "Hold on to the rope, Stephen—don't let go." Then he released his grip on the boy's shoulders.

Quentin and Lucy were both pulling on the rope. Swimming after Stephen, trying to kick off his sneakers at the same time, Troy didn't see the white-tipped crest of water until it closed over his head and almost playfully propelled him back into the rock that had overturned them. The rock was encrusted with barnacles that tore his shirt as though it were paper and rasped his skin like sandpaper. He gasped with pain, swallowed salt water and rose, choking, to the surface.

He was facing Fishhead Island. His knee struck solid granite and pain shot through his leg. Wheezing for air, he saw the second wave just before it slapped him full in the face. It would be silly, he thought, as it spiraled him downwards, to drown so close to shore.

The undertow pulled at him with greedy hands, and for the first time Troy felt real terror. Hot knives of pain were stabbing his lungs; the weight of water over his head was pushing him down, down, down. His ankle banged against a rock. With what presence of mind was left to him, he braced both feet against it and pushed himself upward. His head broke the surface and he saw Quentin standing only a few feet from him. The rope—bright yellow, Troy noticed with preternatural clarity—again snaked through the air. Troy grabbed for it, swallowed another mouthful of water and wrapped the rope round his knuckles. Quentin gave a sharp tug and only moments later Troy's feet found a purchase on the slippery shale bottom.

Quentin guiding him, he staggered out of the water, fell to his knees and coughed up sea water until his throat was raw. Lucy was holding him now, holding him as if she never intended to let go, repeating his name over and over again like a mantra. He heaved himself to a sitting position and through the pain in his chest managed to spit out the one essential question. "Is Stephen safe?"

"He's fine. Oh, God, Troy, I thought you were going to drown in front of my eyes." Her voice rose in panic. "You're bleeding—what happened?"

"Barnacles," he muttered, and looked up. She was white-faced and dry-eyed, and she was trembling all over. "It's okay, just give me a minute."

Then Stephen came between them, butting his body into Troy's. "I wanted to get a shell for the baby," he said in a flood of words. "A special shell. The biggest whelks I ever saw live on Fishhead Island, so that's why I went. It wasn't windy when I left—honestly, it wasn't. I did check because I didn't want to get grounded again. But I got watching the seals and I forgot what the time was and by then the tide had turned and I got really scared."

Breathing was beginning to seem like a more normal occupation, that might go on for some time. Troy said, "If I was your father, you'd be grounded until Christmas—you scared me out of two years' growth." He tilted the boy's chin in fingers that were still not quite steady and looked right at him. "If you're going to be a naturalist, Stephen, you've got to learn the difference between calculated risk and outright danger. And learn it fast, before you either drown me or pull me headfirst down a cliff. Show me the shell.''

With a shamefaced grin Stephen produced a large white shell, whorled and smooth as bone. "Do you think she'll like it?" he asked anxiously.

"I'm sure she will." Not even sure he could stand up, let alone walk, Troy added, "We should go back to the inn before we both catch pneumonia."

Quentin was dragging the boat up the beach. Stephen went to help and Lucy said vehemently, "That boy is a menace. He's enough to put anyone off parenthood."

Troy didn't want to talk about parenthood. "When he and I had our chat yesterday, about the baby, he mentioned getting her a shell and he did look out at the island—I remember that now. But I didn't realize he'd go out there by himself... Lucy, don't be angry with him because he's alive and Michael isn't."

"I'm angry at him because you nearly drowned out there," Lucy said vigorously. "It's got nothing to do with Michael. Are you going to be able to get up?"

"I'm not as sure of the answer to that as I'd like to be," Troy said. Leaning on her shoulder, he pushed himself upright and stood there, wavering a little on his feet. "Any doctor worth his salt would prescribe a hot shower and half a bottle of brandy, don't you think?"

"Not to mention a new shirt," Lucy said, putting an arm round his waist. "Let's go."

Quentin came up beside them, holding Stephen by the hand. "We'll probably get the other boat back at low tide. You want me to take Troy, Lucy?"

"No," she said, "I don't."

Quentin chuckled. "I'll hike Stephen back home, then, and tell Anna what happened. Good thing Keith's gone for the day."

Tears hanging on his lashes, Stephen said, "I didn't mean for you to get hurt, Troy."

The line of trees was dipping up and down, and Troy's knees had the consistency of jellyfish. But Stephen deserved an answer; he was a truthful boy, and no doubt had checked the wind and water before setting off for the island. Leaning a little more of his weight on Lucy, Troy said, "Before you go to sleep tonight, repeat twenty times: I will always remember to keep an eye on the tide. Rule number one for a serious naturalist."

"Okay." Rubbing at the shell, Stephen added, "When Jennifer's older she can go with me. That way there'll be two of us to watch the tide."

"I'd wait a while before you suggest that plan to your mother," Troy advised, grinning at the boy.

Quentin and Stephen took off. More slowly, Lucy and Troy followed. The walk was long enough for each one of Troy's aches and pains to make itself known; he was hobbling by the time they reached the inn. He reached for the back door. But Lucy tightened her grip on his arm and steered him the other way. "Come to my cabin, Troy. You can shower there, and I'll pilfer some brandy from the bar."

He had been dreading climbing the stairs to his room. Nor, he realized, was he in any hurry to be alone. "Bring me some dry clothes, too, would you?"

"Sure." She guided him into the cabin and pulled out fresh towels. "I'll be right back."

Troy stripped off his wet clothes, leaving them in a heap on the floor. There was a long narrow mirror on the back of the bathroom door. He looked at himself without favor, deciding he could have posed as an escapee from *Treasure Island*. His swollen knee was tinged rather prettily with blue and pink, his cheek sported a rope burn, and his ribs were a network of scrapes and cuts from his embrace with the barnacles.

The shower, on balance, probably helped more than it hurt. He was gingerly drying himself off when he heard Lucy moving around in the other room. "Pass me my clothes, please, Lucy?" he asked, winding the towel round his hips.

She opened the door. "I think you should spend the rest of the afternoon in bed," she said, sounding more sure of herself than she looked. "I'll light the fire, and your brandy's poured. Then I want to have a shower, too—even though I was hardly in the water, I'm cold."

It was a measure of Troy's tiredness that all her offer meant was that he could take the weight off his knee. He draped the towel over the rail and, unselfconscious in his nakedness, limped across the room to the bed. She had drawn the curtains; a snifter of brandy stood on the table by the bed. He slid under the covers, took a healthy gulp and said appreciatively, "Courvoisier."

"I steal nothing but the best," Lucy said demurely, her back to him as she tossed shavings and kindling in the stove. Within a few minutes she had a good fire going; she then disappeared into the bathroom. Troy lay back, the cognac tracing a warm path down his throat. He should stay awake, he thought muzzily. He really had to talk to Lucy—time was running out.

Although she'd be here when he woke up—she had the rest of the day off. Maybe she'd be sitting by the fire reading—a picture that gave him considerable pleasure. His lashes drifted to his cheeks and his breathing deepened.

*   *   *

Troy woke from a dream all the more poignant because he had had it many times before. Lucy was in his arms, her naked body curled into his, her breathing wafting his throat. He struggled to free himself, knowing the reality to which he would return: a bed empty other than himself, a house quiet of any sounds except those he himself made. He opened his eyes.

Lucy was in his arms. It had been no dream.

He shook his head and blinked. She was still there. And like a perfect fulfilment of the dream she was naked, her breasts against his chest, her thighs warmly entwined with his, her gray eyes only inches from his face. Gray eyes that were calm and sure of themselves, he noticed, and said with painful truth, "Don't do this to me, Lucy."

As he pushed her away every one of the cuts along his ribs stung as sharply as if he'd had a brush with a Portuguese man-of-war. Drawing a harsh breath, he said, "Go and sit by the fire. Or else I'll have to get out of here."

Her voice sliced to his heart as cleanly as a scalpel. "Troy, I'm exactly where I want to be."

As bright as a flame, and just as fickle, hope flared to life in his breast. He said thickly, "You know how I feel about you, how much I want you—we promised we wouldn't play games with each other."

Very tenderly Lucy reached out her hand and stroked his cheekbone above the raw scrape of the rope burn. "I meant every word I said." Her eyes filled with tears, damping her lashes. "I thought you were going to drown right in front of me—be pulled under and never come up. I've always known that I never stopped loving you or wanting you. In those few seconds when I thought I'd lost you—they felt like hours; I thought they'd never end—I felt such bitter regret, such terrible sorrow... I know I'm not explaining this well.''

"You're doing fine," Troy said, his heart banging against his sore ribs and every muscle as tense as stretched wire.

"All those months I lived in Ottawa I thought I'd never be able to live with you again. Never wake up in the morning in your arms, in our big bed with the sunlight shining between the curtains. Never talk to you half the night—remember how we used to do that? Never make love to you again." Her breath shuddered in her throat. "I can't believe I was so frightened, so off balance, as to cut myself off from my life's blood. Because that's what you are to me, Troy. I can survive without you, I suppose—I've proved that the last year and half. But it's not living. It's only existing, going from day to day, each one the same uniform shade of gray."

Troy said huskily, "Lucy, dear——"

"I'm not finished." Lucy laid one palm to his chest, her eyes widening as she felt the heavy pounding of his heart. "There's more." Two tears overflowed, trickling down her cheeks. "Do you know what else I realized in those few seconds when you were underwater? That I'd never bear any more of your children. That because of Michael, I'd exiled myself from the joy and the love we saw in Anna's face." Unawares, she was pressing her other hand to the flatness of her belly. "That without you I'd be forever after empty in all ways. No husband. No lover. No child. That's what I realized."

Troy took her hand and brought it to his mouth. "I'm not still dreaming?" he said roughly.

"No, this is real." Three more tears spilled from her lashes. "I want to have another child, Troy. Our child. I'll be frightened, I know I will. I'm sure sometimes I'll spend the whole night standing by the crib listening to the baby breathe and praying nothing happens to it. But more than fear there'll be love and fulfilment. I know that now." Her fingers suddenly clenched against his lips. "If you still want another baby...maybe you don't."

"Want one?" Troy kissed her fingers one by one, his eyes brimming with happiness. "Yes, I want another child, Lucy. Maybe even two—how would you feel about that?"

More tears ran in little rivulets down her face. "A dozen," she said, her smile like a rainbow through clouds. "Although perhaps I should reserve the right to downscale that."

He laughed exultantly, pulling her closer. "Lucy, dearest Lucy. It would seem Stephen and the seals have done us an enormous favor."

"I would have got there sooner or later," she mumbled against his chest. "But when you went under for the second time and I thought it was too late—well, it clarified everything. Brought me back to the essentials and made nonsense of my fears. Because no fear could be as great as losing you."

Troy held her close, his face buried in the soft mass of her hair. "I think you'd better pinch me. I'm still not sure whether I'm dreaming or awake."

She lifted her face. "Why don't I kiss you instead?"

For a moment all the old fears raised their ugly heads. "Lucy, if you kiss me you know what'll happen... Maybe we should wait. Maybe you're not ready to risk starting a child now—this soon. Because we have no protection whatsoever."

"I want to make love to you now," Lucy said, stroking his cheek. "And if we're blessed enough to start a baby, that will make me—and, I hope, you—very happy." In sudden fierceness she added, "We've waited long enough, Troy. Too long. I don't want to wait any more."

He said, laughter once more welling up in his chest, "Okay—just don't kick me in the left knee, and watch out for my ribs. Other than that, my darling Lucy, I promise I am in every way more than ready to accommodate you."

Through her tears she was laughing, too. "Shall we put it to the test?"

"Let's," he said, cupping her face in his hands and kissing her with all the love that was in his heart. Against her mouth he whispered, "Now we really have come home."

"I do love you," she said.

Her lips had parted to welcome him, her tongue dancing with his. "I'm drowning again," he murmured. "In happiness this time."

Her hand moved down his belly to hold him where he was indeed ready for her. She said mischievously, "What a way to go."

His voice roughening, Troy said, "Sometimes it was your laughter I missed most of all... Keep doing that and you're going to be in trouble."

"Hurray," said Lucy.

Each caress brought Troy closer to losing control and, paradoxically, closer to a place of absolute safety. It was as if Lucy had set out to show him with her touch that she'd meant every one of her words; she wooed him with open seduction, being gentle with his battered body yet so ardent and unbridled in her need of him that Troy forgot about his sore ribs, his aching knee, and roamed every inch of her body with passionate attention, giving to her and demanding from her without restraint.

It was a voyage both of rediscovery and of re-assurance. The silken perfection of her breasts, her writhing hips, her endlessly beautiful legs—on all of them he left his mark, until she was panting with hunger. "Now," she said, her eyes burning into his, "now, Troy." As he lowered himself on to her her thighs were open to receive him. He touched her delicately, teasing the petals of her flesh, watching her throw her head back and hearing her moan deep in her throat; and he knew that he, no more than she, could not wait any longer.

She was only too ready for him. Troy slid within her, closing his eyes in the sudden rapture of being clasped by her. As she lifted her legs, wrapping them round his thighs, he looked down into the tumult of her eyes and the pared-down beauty of her face and drove into her. Then both of them were thrusting in unison, claimed by the same desperate need for completion. He heard her cry out his name, once, twice, like a wild creature, and let go himself, draining himself inside her in that ecstasy that was like no other, and that gave him life even as it emptied him of it.

Trying to keep most of his weight on his elbows, Troy let his face fall to Lucy's shoulder. Through his ribcage he could feel the frantic race of her heartbeat and against his cheek the tiny puffs of her breath. He said, "I love you, Lucy."

She shifted so she could look at him. "I love you, too."

In quick concern he said, "You're crying again. What's wrong?"

"I'm crying because I'm so happy. This feels so right—I don't understand how I could have stayed away from you for so long. I only hope some day you'll forgive me."

"Lucy," Troy said strongly, "you were a mother who'd lost her firstborn child. That's one of the most terrible things that can happen to a woman, and you dealt with it the best way you knew how. There's no need for forgiveness—I made more than my share of mistakes."

"We'll never forget him," she said.

"How could we? He'll always be part of our lives, and so he should be. But it's time to move on. And I'd like to think we have his blessing for that."

"I'm sure we do." Then, her face as open to him as the pages of a book he had read many times, she said, "You've been so steadfast, Troy, you didn't give up on me... I'll never forget that."

"I'm not sure I had any choice."

"I think you did." With the air of one discovering a profound truth, Lucy said, "Love is amazing, isn't it?"

"Astounding," Troy agreed.

Her eyes flicked to the little alarm clock. "A whole hour before we have to go to dinner."

"How about an aperitif?" he suggested, brushing her breast with his fingertip.

"For a man who could scarcely walk a couple of hours ago, you're doing just fine," Lucy said.

"I am, aren't I?" Troy agreed immodestly.

The aperitif somehow turned into a full meal, as a result of which they were late for dinner. Mrs Mossop looked askance at Lucy's glowing cheeks and frowned disapprovingly at Troy, who had the look of a man who had been well and truly loved. The birders, who had sighted a scissor-tailed flycatcher on one of the posts of the wharf when the boat landed, paid neither Troy nor Lucy the slightest attention.

*   *   *

Nine months later Christopher Stephen moved into the nursery in the big house in Vancouver, and in two years he was joined by his sister, Shannon Lucille. Three years after that, Troy and Lucy took both children to Shag Island, where Stephen, now a skinny adolescent, found them owl feathers among the trees and seashells on the beach. And one afternoon, when Anna was looking after their two children, Lucy and Troy made love on a soft carpet of green moss, where the sun danced on the forest floor and the sea whispered its ancient secrets in their ears.

*   *   *

Look out for Quentin and Marcia's story
in *After Hours*, coming soon!

Coming Next Month

HARLEQUIN **PRESENTS**®

THE BEST HAS JUST GOTTEN BETTER

#1833 THE FATHER OF HER CHILD Emma Darcy
Lauren didn't want to fall in love again—but when she saw Michael all her good resolutions went out the window. And when she learned he was out to break her heart she vowed never to see him again. But it was too late....

#1834 WILD HUNGER Charlotte Lamb
Book Four: *SINS*
Why was Gerard, famous foreign correspondent, following Keira? She could hardly believe he was interested in the story of a supermodel fighting a constant battle with food. No, he wanted something more....

#1835 THE TROPHY HUSBAND Lynne Graham
(9 to 5)
When Sara caught her fiancé being unfaithful, her boss, Alex, helped pick up the pieces of her life. But Sara wondered what price she would have to pay for his unprecedented kindness.

#1836 THE STRENGTH OF DESIRE Alison Fraser
(This Time, Forever)
The death of Hope's husband brought his brother, Guy, back into her life, and left her with two legacies. Both meant that neither Hope nor Guy would be able to forget their erstwhile short-lived affair.

#1837 FRANCESCA Sally Wentworth
(Ties of Passion, 2)
Francesca was used to having the best of everything—and that included men. The uncouth Sam was a far cry from her usual boyfriends, but he was the only man who had ever loved her for what she was rather than what she had.

#1838 TERMS OF POSSESSION Elizabeth Power
Nadine needed money—and Cameron needed a child. His offer was extraordinary—he would possess her body and soul and the resulting baby would be his. But the arrangements were becoming complicated...

HARLEQUIN ⬩ PRESENTS®

brings you the best books
by the best authors!

EMMA DARCY
Award-winning author
"Pulls no punches..."   —*Romantic Times*

Watch for:
#1833 The Father of Her Child
by Emma Darcy

Lauren didn't want to fall in love again—but
when she saw Michael all her good resolutions
went out the window....

Harlequin Presents—the best has just gotten better!
Available in September wherever
Harlequin books are sold.

TAUTH-12

HARLEQUIN PRESENTS®

THIS TIME, FOREVER

THE PAST
Guy had once been the only man
Hope could turn to.

THE PRESENT
Now he was back!

THE FUTURE
And once again Jack's behavior was
pushing Hope into Guy's arms.
Would this time be forever?

Watch for:
#1836 THE STRENGTH OF DESIRE
by Alison Fraser

Available in September wherever
Harlequin books are sold.